Hide Not Thou Thy Face

A.S.Chambers

This story is a work of fiction.
All names, characters and incidents portrayed are fictitious and the works of the author's imagination. Any resemblance to actual persons, living or dead is entirely coincidental.

First published by Basilisk Books in 2020
This edition published in 2024.
Copyright © 2024 Basilisk Books.

All rights reserved. No part of this publication may be reproduced, stored in a retrieval system, or transmitted, in any form or by any means without the prior written permission of the publisher, nor be otherwise circulated in any form of binding or cover other than that in which it is published and without a similar condition being imposed on the subsequent purchaser.

A.S.Chambers asserts his moral right to be identified as the author of this work.

Cover art © 2020 Liam Shaw.

ISBN: 978-1-915679-39-0

Acknowledgements

Many thanks to the long-suffering artistic genius that is
Liam Shaw.
Who would have thought that a werewolf's claw could
have caused so much pain...

Also by A.S.Chambers

Sam Spallucci Series.
The Casebook of Sam Spallucci – 2012
Sam Spallucci: Ghosts From The Past – 2014
Sam Spallucci: Shadows of Lancaster – 2016
Sam Spallucci: The Case of The Belligerent Bard – 2016
Sam Spallucci: Dark Justice – 2018
Sam Spallucci: Troubled Souls – 2020
Sam Spallucci: Bloodline - Prologues & Epilogue – 2021
Sam Spallucci: Bloodline – 2021
Sam Spallucci: Fury of the Fallen – 2022
Sam Spallucci: The Case of The Pillaging Pirates – 2023
Sam Spallucci: Lux Æterna – Due 2024

Short Story Anthologies.
Oh Taste And See – 2014
All Things Dark And Dangerous – 2015
Let All Mortal Flesh – 2016
Mourning Has Broken – 2018
If Ye Loathe Me – 2022
Out of the Depths – 2023
Hear My Scare – Due 2025

Ebook short stories.
High Moon - 2013
Girls Just Wanna Have Fun – 2013
Needs Must - 2019

Novellas.
Songbird – 2019
Bobby Normal and The Eternal Talisman – 2021
Bobby Normal and the Virtuous Man – 2021
Bobby Normal and the Children of Cain – 2022
Bobby Normal and the Children of Cain – 2022
Bobby Normal and The Fallen – 2023
Bobby Normal and the Black Dragon – 2024
Child of Light – Due 2024
Child of Fire – Due 2025

Omnibuses.
Children of Cain - 2019
Macabre Collection: Volume One – 2022
Macabre Collection: Volume Two – 2023
Sam Spallucci Omnibus: Volume One – 2022
Sam Spallucci Omnibus: Volume Two – 2024
The Adventures of Bobby Normal – 2024

Contents

Orion's Hunter

Swarbrick's guts lurched for the umpteenth time.

As a child, he had always struggled with a nervous stomach. Any new experience had seen him cowering in fear, knees knocking, as he tried not to vomit up the contents of his riling and roiling insides.

But then he had taken control of his life, his body. He had beaten any errant nerves into a withering submission as he had grown in stature and developed a hunger to achieve more with his life. He had shunned the usual route of university, scorning those who waved their liberal arts degrees in his face, deciding instead to work his way up from the bottom of the journalism world. What didn't kill him, had its head wrenched from its shoulders as he climbed rapidly through the ranks, trampling over any who dared to block his path. Eventually, his crowning glory was owning his own newspaper, the *Lancaster Chronicle*. He had settled down, albeit somewhat later in life than his peers, married and produced two children. He had lived with his model family out in Slyne-with-Hest, in a nice house in a nice neighbourhood.

Until it had all fallen to pieces.

The damned investigator: Spallucci.

The man had interfered, messed with Swarbrick's son, Billy. Convinced the boy of super-natural mumbo jumbo. Embarrassed Swarbrick in the city and the surrounding area.

It had been the beginning of the end. Janet had left him, taking the kids with her. She had even taken his dog. He had been left with the house and memories that taunted him into the late hours of the night.

But she wasn't going to take his business, he was damned sure of that. His expensive lawyers were working relentlessly to make sure that she didn't get a penny. Not a jot.

Let her starve, he thought. *Let her come crawling back and see just what she's missing.*

And then there was Stone...

Vincent Stone, the poster boy of modern business, riding into Lancaster on his silver steed to right wrongs, create jobs and develop the rundown Quayside area.

Oh yes, that was the *public* image of the modern-day Lord Ashton; affluent and generous to the city. The people didn't know what he was really like, though. Any dissent against his work was quashed or, as in Swarbrick's case, given certain financial incentives to look the other way. Every month an anonymous donation was paid into the otherwise barren coffers of the struggling *Chronicle*, ensuring that local journalists looked the other way as he rode roughshod over building regulations and drove his bold, brash plans through the council's planning committee.

Until enough was enough and the paper magnate could stand no more. The front page last week had been a damning attack on the Quayside development and the imperial stance of Stone himself.

This morning the phone had rung.

His stomach clenched again and he winced.

"Are you okay?"

Swarbrick looked up from his nauseous reverie. For the first time he realised that he wasn't alone in the waiting area, outside the large, ornate wooden door that screamed affluence. There was a woman sat opposite him. She looked early thirties, possessed something which seemed quite remarkable in this day and age; natural blonde hair. It was cut in a fashionable but neat design and, from underneath, dark brown eyes were peering over at him.

"Something I ate," he grumbled. "Nothing to worry about."

A smile touched the corner of the woman's mouth. "I see. It's just that Mister Stone tends to have quite an unsettling effect on most people. It would be understandable if you were nervous."

"Nervous!" The newspaper magnate laughed. "Nothing makes me nervous. Especially jumped up little builders who think they're landed gentry." He frowned. "Why are *you* here?"

"My production company, Celestial Media, are interested in interviewing him for my prime-time television programme. You might have heard of it, *Faces of Today*?"

Swarbrick shrugged. "Not interested in television. *Real* journalism is in the newspapers."

"Ah! I thought I recognised you. It's Hector Swarbrick, isn't it? I applied for a job with you at the *Chronicle* when I was a teenager, fresh out of school."

"Did you get it?"

"No. Best thing that ever happened. Made me the woman that I am today."

Swarbrick harrumphed. "Don't remember you. What's your name, did you say?"

The wooden door opened and a shaggy-haired suit entered the waiting room. "Mister Stone will see you now," he growled at Swarbrick.

The first thing that hit Hector Swarbrick when he entered the inner sanctum of Stone Enterprises was that Vincent Stone had sickeningly good taste. The newspaper magnate had expected the room to be an outlandish statement on nouveau riche extravagance; it should have been dominated by an oversized desk laden with numerous executive toys and be adorned with gaudy postmodern prints hanging from the walls that were, in turn, constructed from faux oak panelling.

Instead, Stone's office was simply understated. The desk sat to one side; a plain affair constructed from an elegantly carved light brown wood. A sofa and a comfortable chair had been placed over in the other corner. The only other items of furniture were two statues standing either side of the panoramic window that overlooked the glorious vista of Morecambe Bay; both bronze, one was a hunter stood with a raised club, the other was an Egyptian-looking composite figure with the head of a dog of some sort atop the muscular body of a man. Again, neither were gaudy nor ostentatious. Both were beautifully cast and bore looks of serenity whilst also seeming to capture implied moments of action. Swarbrick shuddered. The craftsmanship of the statues was without fault and had he come across them in a museum he would have considered them as beautiful objets d'art. But seeing them here, in an otherwise clean cut, modern office, there was just something about the bronzes that chilled him to the core. Their dark contrast to the light airiness of the surrounding room made their sculpted muscles come alive. Their metal eyes peered down at him, like hidden monsters from his childhood, deciding whether or not they should pounce upon him, drag him into the shadows and devour him.

"I see you are admiring my statues." Stone was sat in the comfy chair, tending to a pot of coffee that accompanied a pair of mugs on a small table. "Do you take milk, or do you prefer it as God intended?"

"Sorry?" Swarbrick frowned, thrown immediately off track.

Stone smiled disarmingly and gestured to the coffee table.

"Oh. I see. Black please. No sugar."

"Excellent," the businessman beamed. "I never trust a man who desecrates his coffee. Such a marvellous taste from such a little bean. Why should we pollute it? Come," he gestured to the sofa, "sit. We have much to talk about."

Swarbrick made his way over to the sofa and seated himself down, his eyes not once leaving the man in front of him who sat enjoying the aroma of a deep, black brew. He was everything his posters proclaimed; blonde, finely chiselled, immaculately dressed, handsome. The poster boy for a new generation of self-made men. His suit was perfectly cut and neither rumpled nor creased as he leaned back in the armchair. His shirt fit perfectly over his obviously well-toned physique and a small pair of green-stoned cufflinks fastened sleeves that were the perfect length for his arms.

Swarbrick could not help but feel the flush of jealousy heat his cheeks. It just wasn't fair! He had slaved his entire life to get where he was, yet Stone was quite literally an overnight phenomenon.

Perhaps that was why he had written such a damning article?

An article that had seen him summoned to the headmaster's study for a severe dressing down.

Swarbrick was aware of movement behind him. The goon who had shown him in was stood with his back to the only door into the room. He was just above average height, sporting a mop of shaggy blonde hair and a taciturn tongue, his eyes gazing easily off out of the window. He looked more or less like a normal guy, just passing the time of day, but Swarbrick was no fool. He knew exactly what this was.

It was a very dangerous situation.

"They're Orion and Anubis," Stone commented, referring back to the two statues. "Both were important deities to the Egyptians."

"I thought Orion was Greek," Swarbrick frowned as he reached for an offered cup of coffee.

The cup paused, hovered just out of comfortable reach. Swarbrick looked over at Stone's hard blue eyes and, for an instant, he thought he was a dead man. Then the businessman smiled affably and the saucer touched the journalist's fingers which grabbed it quickly to obscure any tremble.

"I see your reputation for being perceptive is well-earned. You are quite right, Orion *was* Greek, but the constellation in the night sky was venerated by the Egyptians. They initially referred to it as Sah before it sort of evolved into Osiris. Did you know that the pyramids at Giza align perfectly with it?"

Swarbrick sipped the coffee in order to wet his parched mouth before answering, "You learn something new every day."

"Indeed you do," mused Stone, relaxing back into his chair, not a care in the world, just two chaps chatting. "Indeed you do.

"Do you know what I learned the other day?"

Swarbrick's cup froze in front of his lips.

"I learnt that you don't seem to regard my Quayside redevelopment as very honourable.

"I was wondering why that might be?" He sipped his coffee. "Beautiful. The beans for this come from Peru, you know. Imagine that? Small brown beans cultivated and raised on a hillside near Machu Pichu itself, ending up here in this very room in these little cups, providing you and me with pleasurable bursts of flavour.

"It's amazing what effect little things can have, isn't it?

"Just like words."

Swarbrick shifted on the sofa. He seriously wanted to be somewhere else right now.

"*Thief*, that was one word, wasn't it? *Liar* was another. *Charlatan*." Stone sighed. "Very saddening. Very saddening indeed, especially as your little paper benefits from my generosity.

"Mind you, those words are somewhat water off a proverbial duck's back to me. I've heard them all before, many times, in other little cities. Do you know what little word hurt me most, though, Mr. Swarbrick?"

Swarbrick's head juddered from left to right.

"*Unwelcome*. This chap here, the one drinking my beautiful coffee from the hillsides of Peru, called me unwelcome, Chris. Can you believe it?"

Swarbrick heard a sigh from the goon on the door.

"Tell me, Hector, what makes me unwelcome in your fair city? I'd really like to know."

The newspaper owner's stomach lurched. He was five again, terrified of the monsters in the closet. He had been listening to Douglas, his older brother, telling him horror stories when their parents had been out. The gruesome tales had turned him a nauseous shade of pale. If he opened the door then the beast would crawl out, its teeth glinting in the bright moonlight. It would pace across the bedroom floor, drool suspended from its long fangs, hunger in its dark eyes.

"Hector? Are you in there?"

Swarbrick's head snapped up to the here and now. "You... You've used outside contractors when we have local builders who... who could perform a more than adequate job. Not once were local people consulted on what you're building. You're just throwing up whatever you feel like and plastering a facade of public relations over it." He thought he was going to be sick.

Stone's bright blue eyes studied him in the ensuing silence.

He sipped his coffee.

He placed the cup and saucer down and leant forward, smiling. "Now, Hector." The businessman's voice was smooth, soothing, yet Swarbrick saw something else entirely in his sharp eyes. "You know that's just a gross misrepresentation, isn't it? Yes, I've used outside contractors. I've used my own teams which I *always* use. I *know* them. I *trust* them. Let's face it, Hector, trust is everything, isn't it? Without trust, how can we progress as a society? As for not consulting... How on earth do you think I got planning permission? The plans were there for all to see. The old Williamson works had been derelict for so long, something needed to be done with them. I am rejuvenating a dead area of town. I am providing houses that are sorely needed. *Real* houses, Hector, not jerry-built student flats the likes of which other companies seem to be spewing up all over the place. Not only this, but I'm bringing amenities to this neck of the woods. There will be shops, a doctor's surgery and a school. A school, Hector!" he beamed. "You of all people should appreciate that. You *are* still chair of governors at Edmund Campion?"

Swarbrick gave a minuscule shake of his head. Along with his marriage, Spallucci's interference had also scuppered his prestigious post as chair of governors. There had been mutterings, whispers that he was a liability. It had been suggested that perhaps he wanted to spend more time with his family. Prevent it from fracturing. Fat lot of good that had done.

Stone sat back and shrugged. "Ah, what a shame. Education is such an important thing in life, isn't it?

"And that's what I need you to do, now Hector; educate your readers. You'll go back to your newspaper and retract that article you printed last week. You'll keep your side of our little agreement and I'll keep your provincial little rag afloat, making sure that you are able to pay all those expensive divorce lawyers you have in your employ.

"You'll describe how you were misinformed. You'll talk about our friendly little chat here. You'll tell them all about the wonderful things my development will bring the city, won't you?"

Hector's head was slumped down. He nodded without even looking up.

Stone clapped his hands together. "Splendid! Tell you what, let's seal the deal with a photo. Won't that look marvellous? Right on the front page of tomorrow's edition? Chris, grab my phone, will you?"

The guard by the door picked up Stone's device from the desk and fiddled with the controls.

Stone encouraged Swarbrick from the sofa and positioned him by the statue of Anubis. "Marvellous. Perhaps we should be shaking hands? What do you think? Won't that send the correct message?"

Hector, broken and beaten without so much as a punch being delivered, did exactly as he was told. He stood, he posed, he shook hands.

"Splendid, Chris. Let me see. Oh, yes. I do like that." Stone typed on the phone and a small whooshing noise came from the handset. "There we go. All sent. You'll get that sorted this afternoon, won't you, Hector? Jolly good. Right then, I'd better not detain you. Off you go," he smiled.

Swarbrick's feet led him out of the room and the door closed shut behind the shadow of a man.

Vincent Stone watched as the solid door closed behind the broken magnate. In his ever-calculating head, varying permutations were forming and reforming. Outcome after outcome was examined and dismissed until he finally settled on the one that he knew was necessary.

The smile left his face.

He walked over to a painting on the wall of his office. Quite expressionist in style, to the uniformed eye, it was swathe after swathe of writhing, undulating masses of browns and greys seeming to surround a bright green light. To the educated, informed mind, it told a very clear story.

"Chris, I think we need to take out a certain amount of insurance concerning Mr. Swarbrick," the tycoon pondered as he swung the framed canvas to one side and unlocked the safe that was hidden behind.

"Very good, Mr. Stone."

"You're comfortable using this now?"

"Yes, Mr. Stone."

"You're sure? I don't want any mistakes. This has to be quick. Precise." He pulled a leather sack out of the safe and slid its contents into his finely manicured hand. The hemispherical stone emitted its ethereal green glow and he moaned in pleasure. "Make sure to sink right down into its power. Let it guide you."

"Yes, Mr. Stone. As you showed me."

Vincent Stone, builder of empires, nodded, his eyes a hazy green in the light from the gemstone. "Good. Tonight. Do it tonight. I will know if he has done as he has been instructed." Carefully, reverentially, he slid the stone back into the sack and replaced it in the safe. Once it was locked away, he took a sharp breath, smoothed his blonde locks and turned to face his PA.

"Oh, I've been meaning to ask, how's our operative getting on?"

Dootson seemed to repress a sigh as he replied, "She seems fine."

Stone paused as he walked back to his desk. "*Seems*? That does not sound very positive. Is there a problem."

"With respect, she is somewhat abrasive. Her colleagues have taken to her all well and good, but..."

"The DCI?"

Dootson nodded. "She claims that he doesn't trust her. She says that he's constantly putting her down."

Stone sank down into his luxurious office chair

and steepled his fingers in thought. After a moment he said, "You have concerns that she is a loose cannon? That she is jumping at shadows, perhaps?"

The PA's head inclined slightly to the left. "Maybe. It's hard to tell."

Stone leaned back and looked his assistant square in the eyes. "Then we shall just have to keep a tight leash on her, won't we? As for now, could you please send in Ms. Adamson?"

"Future of city set in stone."

Swarbrick slammed the lid of his laptop shut and dumped the device next to him on the sofa. He couldn't bring himself to look at the rest of tomorrow's front page. It was garbage, utter garbage and it sickened him. How had he let himself be manoeuvred into printing it? Stone was a parasite. He had drifted in from God alone knew where down south, jingling his seemingly bottomless pockets and had half the city reaching multiple orgasms over his plans to *rejuvenate* the old quayside.

Yes, the Williamson works had been derelict as long as anyone could remember.

Yes, there was a chronic housing shortage if you weren't some spotty, entitled undergrad.

Yes, Stone seemed to be the only person willing to do something about it.

But at what cost?

The newspaper owner's stomach turned again, just as it had when he had been waiting outside the businessman's office. There was something rotten about the man. He didn't know what, but he just felt it.

And he knew that he wasn't the only one who felt likewise.

Rumour had it that the city's detective chief inspector had been probing into the man's background. DCI Jitendra Patel was not a man to be trifled with. If he thought there was trouble, then there was indeed trouble.

So, Swarbrick had tried to shine a light on Stone's hidden dark side. He had pointed out all the things that were bound to get the locals up in arms and brandishing the proverbial pitchforks. Instead there had been letters, emails and phone calls, all demanding a retraction of the claims against the good name of the city's modern-day James Williamson.

Then there had been the summons to the office of Stone.

It was over. There was nothing more that he could do now.

On the television, quietly chatting away in the corner, was some sort of documentary. It showed a big, bearded archaeologist striding through the ruins of some sort of ancient civilisation. Swarbrick yawned and flicked the set off. He needed to go to bed and put this wretched day to an end.

Chris Dootson stood over on the opposite side of Sefton Close, a quiet cul-de-sac in the respectable village of Slyne-with-Hest. He watched the flickering of a television screen dim to nothing and sighed.

It was almost time.

Swarbrick would be getting ready to retire to bed.

He would be sleepy. He would be vulnerable.

In the cold winter night, the former aerial repairman, now PA to one of the richest men in England, looked up into the night sky. His view of the stars was far from perfect (street lights caused far too much pollution), but the unmistakable figure of Orion dominated the sky as it rose up into the heavens, its club raised high over its head.

He felt a slight throbbing sensation from his jacket pocket and pulled out the plain leather bag. Its material felt warm to the touch, as if it contained something alive, something vital. Nervously, he ran his tongue over his lips before looking up into the firmament once more. There, rising over the horizon was a clear crescent moon.

Not a full one. A *crescent* moon.

Chris left the footpath and rounded a shadowy corner where he drew the stone from its bag. At once, his head erupted into a cacophony of song with unintelligible words. He was aware of three sounds sung over and over in quick repetition, but he could not make them out. It was as if they were being sung in a foreign tongue from a distant land. But he knew what they wanted.

They were hungry.

He drew the stone over his neck and let it feed.

Deep down, into his heart, he let the stone race. It chased his pulsing blood flow, the drumming of its hunter's paws matching the time of his beating pulse. Chris felt his knees weaken as if he were being encompassed by a powerful deluge. Massive waters from abyssal depths rose up around him, such power that mere mortals were not meant to possess.

But he was no mere mortal.

He was far more than that.

Inside him, the wolf stirred, anxious to be awake. It growled and snarled as it swam to the surface through the flood. It joined the hunt and raced along his veins, clawing its way through the human that rapidly began to recede.

Dootson felt his body twist, morph, alter beyond recognition, and there, in the light of the crescent moon, the wolf howled to the hunter above.

Swarbrick paused with his foot on the first stair of his staircase. Had he heard a dog outside in the street? He was sure that there had been a howl.

Did dogs howl like that?

He turned and walked back into the hallway, his front door before him.

His dog Dooby had never sounded quite like that. This had sounded like an altogether larger animal.

A monster.

Swarbrick ignored the voice from over forty years previous. He was a grown man, not a scared little child.

The only monsters he knew wore suits.

He continued to stare at his front door.

There was a noise. It came from outside.

Swarbrick was suddenly aware that he had stopped breathing. Unable to move, he stood frozen to his thick Persian rug.

The noise came again. It was a scratching sound. There was something on the other side of the door.

Someone, not something: he told himself. "Who's there?" he shouted, his voice as fearsome as he could manage.

There was a scratching again and movement. Swarbrick watched as the vertical letter flap fluttered and snapped. He took a step backwards. The flap moved again. This time, something came through. An oversized paw pushed through, holding the flap open.

Swarbrick's jaw fell as he observed an eye peering through into his hallway.

It wasn't a human eye.

The flap snapped shut and there was an almighty bang as the something hit the door, causing it to shudder in its frame. This broke Swarbrick's paralysis and he darted up the stairs. It was a firm door, solid oak. He had every confidence that it would hold against whatever was trying to break through, but he wanted to be as far away from it as possible.

He darted up the stairs and slipped on the carpet as another crashing slammed into the door. A pitiful noise escaped his lips and he pulled himself up the rest of the stairs on his hands and knees. When he reached the landing, he heaved himself back up onto his feet and shot into his bedroom. Once in there, he slammed the door shut and heaved the large king size bed in position as a barricade.

There was no way that anything could reach him now.

The wolf that contained the man stood back from the door and listened with its acute hearing to the sounds of feet scrambling up the staircase. It nodded to itself and clung to the shadows as it made its way round to the back of the large, detached house.

The garden round the rear was private. Nothing overlooked it. The man in the wolf had discovered this when he had visited earlier, before his prey had returned home. He had taken his time to wander around a sheltered hunting ground, planning every move that he would take that evening once he had transformed.

The wolf now looked up the rear wall of the building. Its sensitive ears could make out its prey scurrying around in the dark of its bedroom, where it thought it was safe. The bedroom was on the upper floor of an extension to the main body of the house. There was no attic space above it, just a roof. The man inside the wolf was at home on roofs.

The wolf containing the man gripped its paw-like hands around a drain pipe and heaved itself upwards.

The middle-aged man who owned the local newspaper sat curled up in the corner of his bedroom, his eyes fixed on the door that was located behind the bed of his failed marriage. In his mind's eye he saw the door splinter and crack open, the monster from his childhood closet breaking in, its teeth wickedly sharp and its eyes ferociously cruel.

He pictured it clambering towards him, over his futile barricade, its claws stretched out to snag him and eviscerate him, dragging his bedding in its unstoppable wake.

His brother had been right. There were monsters - creatures with unspeakable names from distant nightmares that came for you when you least expected it. They lurked in the back of your closet, their eyes watching you as you came and went. They waited quietly, patiently, feeding off your fear until they had been strengthened by this appetiser, then they threw the door open and pounced.

As Swarbrick's wide eyes stayed fixed on his portal of doom, his ears picked up a noise from another direction.

Above him.

He dragged his eyes away from the bedroom door up to the Velux skylight in the ceiling above him. There framed in the night sky, with the crescent moon behind him, loomed the monster. Swarbrick tried to scream as the creature eased the window out of its frame: the window that the PA dressed as an aerial repairman had unfastened earlier on that afternoon in broad daylight. His voice hitched in his throat as the giant wolf dropped down lightly in front of him.

His throat paralysed in fear, the newspaper magnate was unable to scream any final words, not that there was anyone there to hear him except for his killer.

Chris Dootson, former aerial repairman, lover of the night sky, personal assistant to the most powerful man currently residing in Lancaster, member of the Bloodline of Abel, walked calmly out of the front door of 12, Sefton Close. He had done as he had been asked and that deeply troubled him.

What else was he capable of?

He walked around the corner to where his van was parked just a few streets away, climbed in and drove off into the night.

Angler Fish

Well, this is quite the predicament, isn't it? Who would have thought, just a week ago, that we would find ourselves here, the two of us, alone?

Forever.

I know you don't say much, but I think that's one of the things that I really cherish about you. I always have done, right from the start.

Along with that shining red hair of yours, so bright and vibrant in the summer sun. Natural, not out of a bottle. It always caught the bright rays and glittered, shimmered with such vitality.

Shame I can't see it anymore now.

But I get ahead of myself.

Let's start at the beginning, shall we?

I didn't know I was going to see you that day. How could I? But I didn't even have an inkling when I woke up that morning. It was just the normal routine; wake up, out of bed, fifty push-ups, brisk shower, healthy muesli, polish my collection of knives, watch the morning news. The same as every other day.

It wasn't until I was sipping a delightful little espresso outside that hipster joint in town that I realised this particular day was going to be the start of something special. It was just coming up to ten past twelve and the fiery summer sun was bright and glorious, smiling on both the virtuous and the damned alike, when you glided past. I vividly remember my first sight of you even though I didn't catch your face. Like I said before, the first thing that struck me was that gorgeous russet hair, flame-like in the noontime sun. It was loose and flowing, carefree; so different to the boring, mundane workers and shoppers who trudged along around you. It bounced against your bare shoulders as you sauntered past. My espresso cup paused halfway to my mouth as all I could do was sit and stare. Those red locks were such a vibrant contrast to your delic-ate white dress with the dark blue flowers. You know the one. The dress that looks like it's crafted from the finest china. So smooth that it has to be touched, stroked, smashed.

I lay my forgotten coffee on the table, scraped the legs of my metal chair against the paving slabs and followed you down the street, the reassuring weight of my knife pressing against my side, where it was concealed inside my lightweight summer jacket.

I didn't walk too close. That's never a good idea; it gives people the wrong idea and they think you're crazy. So, I held back, trailing you through the lunchtime crowd of panini-munching plebs that were completely unaware of the beauty that graced their streets.

I was able to keep track of you as your bright locks flashed through the lunchtime hubbub, a bright punctuation in the mundane world.

But it was because of the mundane world that I lost you that day. There were just too many of them swimming helter-skelter in the currents of their pointless lives and after a while I lost track of you.

Perhaps you had entered a shop?

Perhaps you had turned off the high street?

Perhaps you had ascended back up to the heavenly paradise that had sent you to bring beauty to this drab, boring world?

Whatever the reason, I was not pleased at all. I felt a sickening loss in the pit of my stomach as I stormed my way home that afternoon.

I eviscerated a cat to relieve my rage.

It just wasn't the same.

I had to see you again. I needed to know more about you: what was your name; what was your taste in music; what did your heart feel like in my clenched fist? So, I returned to the hipster place the next day. The barista made polite conversation and I smiled whilst I imagined scalping off his pathetic man bun.

Fortunately, no one had occupied the chair in which I had been seated the previous day. I took this as a sign from God and positioned myself there just before twelve.

Just as the Town Hall's clock struck midday, the lunchtime rush commenced its daily ritual. Worshippers of cheap junk food piled out of their places of work and scurried reverentially to their bright, tacky temples.

My heart pounded against the hard steel pressing heavy against my chest.

Would you come?

If you did, would I see you through this disgusting display of modern detritus and greed?

I felt the palms of my hands start to sweat and my throat began to constrict with nerves. I *had* to see you – my soul ached just for another tantalising glimpse of your purity. The pit of my stomach started to lurch and I sipped from the coffee in a vain attempt to stabilise the unsettling sensation.

Then, over the rim of the tiny cup, I caught a flash of fiery red - the glow of an angel.

I slammed the cup down onto the table, causing brown liquid to splash up and over its sides. In my morass I had almost missed you! Pushing my chair back, I made to follow you once more but the lunchtime crowds seemed even busier than the day before. As I struggled to swim against their banal current, I overheard them babbling about mundane lives that did not concern me. They were an abhorrence, a distraction designed to prevent me from reaching you.

One fat, flaccid woman scowled at me as I shoved her wobbling body out of my way. I ignored her, knowing that she was not worthy of my attention. A spotty youth found himself shoved into the back of a muscular brute who turned and roundhoused him squarely in the face. I made the mistake of letting my attention slip as my tongue wetted my lips at the sight of droplets of blood showering the scorched pavement.

When I looked up, you were gone.

My eyes hopelessly scanned the flow of the crowd, desperate for a glimpse of your hair or your dress, the same as yesterday's, but all around me was hurt and horror.

You were nowhere to be seen.

That afternoon a woman spent vain hours trying to find her little poodle that she had carelessly let off its lead.

The third day saw me in a vile temper.

I returned to the hipster joint but didn't even bother to purchase a drink. I just grabbed my seat outside, sat and waited for you to pass.

My knife burnt hot against my chest. I could taste its hunger. Twice now it had been deprived of its feast. Twice it had been insulted, its clean steel sullied with the insides of lesser creatures.

It desired to feast on purity, on light.

I could not deny it.

"Hey, dude. You need to buy a drink if you're gonna, like, sit here."

"I'm waiting for someone. Go away," I snapped. The man bun freak scurried off inside. He knew he was no match for me as I keenly observed the building crowd.

I *would* find you today.

I *would* follow you.

I *would* let my knife feast on you.

And there you were, walking away from me, down the middle of the street - red hair, porcelain dress.

And, as my eyes located you and I rose from my seat, you paused, just for a moment. You knew that I was there. You felt the bond that we shared and you wanted me to follow you.

So, I did.

Oblivious to all around me, I pursued you through the centre of town. This time there were no distractions, no pitiful obstructions. You were the one and only thing in my field of vision, my mouth so broad in a grin that it almost did not fit on my face.

You turned a corner and headed past that large shopping centre that they built some years ago, the one that is half empty, and I kept pace. You knifed through the dazed lunchtime crowd and flitted away from the main flow. I never once lost sight of that flaming red hair. I longed to twist it through my fingers, feel its softness against my blade.

My stomach growled in hunger as the two of us crossed over a busy road, away from the shops. I was a breath behind you now. I could smell your perfume; sweet, intoxicating. Were I to reach out, I could touch your skin and the sensation would be electric.

The sun beat down as we threaded our way up a hill, past the theatre that used to be a church and you darted quickly down the shadowy alley that runs behind it.

This was the moment that I had been waiting for.

This was the time that would bring me my feast.

I reached into my jacket and drew out my knife. A heavy, comforting hilt and a twenty centimetre, finely polished blade, it was one with my hand as I turned into the darkened alley.

Where you stood waiting, your back to me.

You knew that I was there and you welcomed your fate. You knew that we were linked, our special lives bound together in a beauty that the mundane world could never know.

I drew up behind you, carefully placing my footsteps so as not to startle you, cause you to flee at the last moment.

Then you turned.

And I saw your face.

Your porcelain skin split in two down the bridge of your thin nose and writhing tentacles shot out from inside your head. They wrapped themselves around me, squeezing my arms to my sides and gagging my mouth. I felt myself wrenched off my feet and dragged silently into your open maw. I inhaled a sweet scent through my nostrils as I began to hyperventilate and suddenly, the world I knew, one of pain and loss, was left behind.

There was darkness as I was transported somewhere else, then a dim light seeped into my vision and a dull pulse vibrated behind me as I came to, warm, loving tentacles holding me fast against a soft, muscular wall.

It is a warm place where I am now, deep inside you.

We will be together forever.

Just you and me.

And finally, I have found peace.

Infernal Reunion

So, erm, yeah, hi. I suppose this must be, you know, kind of weird. Is your coffee okay? I don't drink those milky ones. Not my cup of tea. Invented by monks, you know. Way, way back. Centuries ago. They were jerks. I mean, come on, who would put milk in coffee? Why? Just why? You lose all the flavour.

Oh, yeah. Sorry.

It's just, you know, I don't really dig the whole monk vibe. Not my kind of guys.

Obviously.

Haha! Ah, yeah. No, it's totally cool. No one can see what I *really* look like. I mean, *Jesus*! Can you imagine if they could? They would so totally freak out. Probably get their little waxed goatees in a bunch before pissing their Fairtrade cotton underwear. It would be so hysterical. No, it's just you who can see the horns and shit. Just you.

Your mum? No, not at first. Not when we first met. She saw me like they all do. Just a regular guy. But I saw her. Oh, yes. She was so pretty. I'll never forget the night in the nightclub – Raffles, it was called. It was supposed to be a work gig. I'd been sent there for this famous celeb. I was under instructions that I was to turn her and bring her down. That's my department: acquisitions. It's kinda fun. Hard work, a lotta research and swotting up, but it's well worth it when you get out in the field. It's all in the prep. No prep and the job goes south very quickly. Anyway, this celeb was a right case. On screen she was all, "Oh, look at me and my good works. I go over to Africa and kiss fly-infested children." Yet, to the crew members, she was a real bitch. An utter diva. If her latte wasn't just so, she'd throw it in her PA's face. If the set was too hot, she'd storm off to her trailer. That sorta crap. So, my superiors said to me that she was ripe for acquiring. I'd done all my research, found out her weaknesses (guys in a sharp tux) and was just homing in for the kill, when I noticed someone sat on her own in the club. She looked so pretty, in a *natural* kind of way – not trying so hard with all the slap and putty and crap. So, I just had to go and talk to her. Well, you know, one thing leads to another and nine months later she rings me and says that she's had a kid.

Yeah, you.

She took it rather well when I told her what I was. She was very understanding. She agreed that it probably wouldn't be best for me to be in your life back then. My boss had hard balls and was constantly on my back about acquiring more and more souls. If he'd found out that I had a kid...

Anyway. Enough about that. Tell me what you do. Your mum says school's going great.

Art? Awesome! I can't draw for toffee. I've *been* painted numerous times, but I just can't see how they do it? I mean all those fine details, especially around the tail.

Ah, yeah. Practice. I guess that's it. I thought it was just a bucket-load of hallucinogens, but I guess practice actually makes far more sense.

Oh, no, no, no! I didn't mean that I thought *you* were doing drugs. Dear God, no. It's just these artists back in the Middle Ages, I mean they were... You know... There was this one guy who I'd been sent to acquire who got so pumped about the idea that he said he just had to sculpt me. Now, I'd never been sculpted before, so I was quite flattered. The guy was working in clay and built this figurine about *so* high. Took him the best part of a week and I have to say that he really captured me. The horns had the right curve; he had the menacing scowl; he made me look totally ripped. But then there was my, *you know*... Now, I guess I should have seen it coming. I mean, all these dudes I get sent after have their own little peccadillos. That's what flags them up as useful. Anyway, when he fashioned junior, so to speak, I think he got a bit carried away. I mean, it was as long as my leg!

Oh God! I'm sorry. Let me get a napkin for that.

Sorry about that. I guess I'm just not really used to small talk. Work doesn't really encourage it. It's all: go in, bag the soul, get out.

You okay?

Yeah, I'm sorry. I guess I *am* being a bit weird...

Oh, yeah. I almost forgot. I bought you a gift. Here you are. I hope you like it.

What? You're not really into unicorns? Oh. I thought all girls loved unicorns.

Ah, yeah. Okay. When they're six, not sixteen. Okay.

You want another coffee?

No.

Okay.

Is it me or is it hot in here?

Do you come to this place a lot?

Okay. It just, well, I can't help but notice that they all look rather *different* to you, you know?

No, no, that's a *good* thing. I mean look at them all. They're all being so infernally righteous in what they wear and what they're talking about. It's all, "Oh yah, I so love the smell of atrophied quinoa, mhmm? Yah, it's just far more ethical that way. Excuse me while I bleed into my reusable Cherokee hair tampon."

Hehe. Yeah, you know what I mean, don't you?

What? No way! That's brilliant. So, you dated a guy who used to work here and he said that the coffee isn't organic Fairtrade as advertised? Ha! I knew I could taste the blood of innocents in my espresso.

Listen, tell you what. Just for you, I could, you know, cause a bit of mayhem. I've got a knife. It's a really nice knife. Had it centuries now. It wouldn't take long and no one would miss any of these jerks.

No? Oh, okay. Well, if you change your mind, just let me know.

Cool.

This is good, isn't it? I'm glad you asked your mum about me. She sent me photos every birthday, you know? I've watched you grow up.

Yes, I've even got ones of you wearing those orthodontic braces.

No, don't be embarrassed. I've seen Victorian teeth. Trust me, they were a damn sight worse.

What? What's the matter?

No, it's not nothing. You've gone tense and your aura has turned a muddy brown. Something's upset you. Was it something I said?

No, no, come on. Tell me. It's not nothing. We were doing so well.

Yeah, I see him. The tall poseur in the tweed jacket with elbow patches.

Oh.

When?

Shit.

Does your mum know?

Why didn't you tell her?

Okay. I can see that. Hey, hey, come on. There's no need for tears.

Not when you can get even.

There's always my knife.

Sure we can. Right here right now.

No. No one will know it was us. They'll still be watching us sat here all daughter and Saturday afternoon dad.

But he *deserves* it.

No, there won't be any blood. It'll be like he just had a heart attack or a stroke. Something normal. Something explainable.

Well having a heart attack or stroke does tend to do that to you, sweetie. But it'll be quick and over in a flash.

You've got to live with what he did to *you* for the rest of your life.

Good girl. Okay. Here it is.

Yeah, I said it was nice, didn't I. This guy back in Babylon made it for me. I love the way it curves; it catches the light just right.

That's right. It doesn't feel as heavy as it looks. I have no idea how he managed that. Like I said, artwork – not my thing. Okay. Come on. Let's do this.

No, no. You take it. It's *your* revenge here. Think about what he did.

There we go. That's it. Your aura's all red now with little fiery black bits. That's my girl. Come on. That's right, we just stand behind him.

No, I promise. No one can see us. Look at our table.

Yeah. Cool, isn't it. Now, just lift the dagger. There you go. Can you feel its song?

That's right, that little whisper in your ears. It enjoys what it does. It lives for it. Now, just here, between the ribs and into the heart.

That's it! Fantastic! Good girl! Whoa, look at him drop.

Yeah, I can see. Must have had a full bladder, the jerk.

I know. It does, doesn't it. Gives you that warm glow deep inside.

What was that? Some girls in your maths group called you fat?

Aw, I think you're gonna make your old man very proud.

The Day The Alien Came

We were bored, Henry and I. We had finished playing with Petey, Henry's old dog that dribbled and drooled whenever it got overexcited, and we had left him in the garage while we went and sat on the front doorstep drinking flat lemonade. It was flat because we had poured it out of its bottle three hours ago before we had started playing with the elderly dog, then we had completely forgotten about it. The tepid drink may have lacked fizz but we were both incredibly thirsty, so glugged it down with welcome relief.

There was a clattering sound from around the side of the house. I looked at Henry; he looked at me. His mum wasn't home and we knew it couldn't be Petey. So, who could it be? Henry scooped up his mum's old video camera, focussed it on himself and narrated into the lens, "We've just heard a mysterious noise and are going to investigate." He likes that dramatic stuff. Not my thing really, so I just leave him to it.

We pulled ourselves off the step and ventured around the side of the semi-detached house, Henry filming as we went. I have to say that what we found was quite unexpected. There, crouching down behind the recycling bins was an alien.

I'm not kidding you, it really *was* an alien. This isn't like the time that Maddie Tompkins said that she was pregnant in year five; I'm not making it up like she did. She just lies about anything to get attention because her parents used to have really important jobs, but now they're broke. There really was an alien there. Henry kept filming to prove it too.

The thing peered at us from around the bins. It was grey-skinned, about my height and had big black eyes that kept blinking in the bright sunshine.

"Hey!" called Henry, "You okay?"

The alien just stared at him.

I rolled my eyes like I see them do on the telly. "He doesn't speak English, dumbass!"

Henry frowned. "What? You mean he's a migrant? My mum keeps saying they're coming over here from all over the place, claiming benefits and taking our jobs."

I practiced my eye rolling again - a crucial skill for dealing with the growing number of idiots in society. Henry was not the brightest kid in year six. He has a table all to himself so he can't hit anyone and has special lessons when the rest of us have PE. I like him though. His mum lets him do what he wants and they have a big garden.

Plus, there's his garage.

"Whatever." I eased myself forward, towards the alien. I was very careful in case it shot death rays from its eyes like they do in the movies. Every time it blinked I felt my heart skip a beat, but I didn't tell

Henry. He would have called me a wimp. What the hell was I supposed to do now? Henry was busy getting all this on video so it was up to me to talk to our visitor.

But how?

I reached into my pocket and pulled out a soft Mars bar. I had been saving it for later, but hey ho. Being careful not to take my eyes off the alien, I slowly unwrapped the chocolate. I was careful not to make any sudden moves as I didn't want him to think the chocolate bar was an alien-killing device. Then I put the exposed end in my mouth and bit off a chunk. I made a big show of just how tasty it was. I went, "Mmmmmm..." licked my lips and rubbed my stomach, all that sort of stuff. Then, I held my arm out and offered the alien the rest of the bar. Its big eyes blinked three times as it stared at the chocolate, then slowly it extended a long, three-fingered hand in my direction.

My heart was going insane now and I was starting to regret drinking all the lemonade as I really needed to pee, but I kept my nerve and prayed quietly that he didn't take my hand as well as the Mars bar. He carefully gripped the chocolate and pulled it from my hand, leaving my fingers thankfully intact. My heart slowed down a bit as the alien held the chocolate up to his face and bit off the end. Its cheeks moved back and forth as it chewed, then it stopped, looked at the rest of the bar and shoved it all in, wrapper and all.

"Cool!" Henry whispered from behind. "Get it to do something else."

Like I said before, Henry has a really big

garden. His dad used to be some sort of money guy and, when he walked out, his mum got a shed load of cash which she was quite happy to spend. One of the ways she spent it was on their garden. She put a load of stuff in there for Henry to play with. One such thing was a big adventure playground structure. There were ropes to climb, wobbly bridges to walk across and a hell of a long slide.

It was quite hard to get the alien up to the top of the slide. His legs were quite short and he struggled to climb the ladder but I helped him up by shoving my shoulder under his fat, wobbly behind and soon we were stood at the top. Henry was down below with his video camera.

"This is fun," I said to the alien, even though I knew it didn't have a clue as to what I was saying. "Watch me." I climbed onto the top of the slide and pushed myself off, screaming while I slid down as if it was a roller coaster.

Panting hard, I rolled off the bottom and gestured for the alien to follow me. Its big, dark eyes blinked as it positioned itself at the top of the slide and looked carefully at its three fingered hands that gripped the polished sides. Then its head turned and looked down at me. I waved my fingers, beckoning him down and it pushed off.

I thought that *I* had screamed loudly...

The noise that came from its mouth was like a finger rubbing down the largest possible soapy plate in the sink. I flinched and automatically covered my ears. Henry almost dropped his camera.

When it got to the bottom, the alien stood up, looked back at the slide and ran back to the ladder which it climbed a lot easier the second time.

It slid down again...

Again...

Again...

Again...

After the fifth time, I felt like my ears were going to bleed.

"This isn't fun anymore," Henry complained. His mouth was turned down like old Petey's used to when he was miserable. It was as if he had been promised a new slipper to chew on, then had it snatched away at the last minute.

Our new toy was not what we had expected.

"I'm bored, too." I cringed as the alien started another clamber up the ladder. "Let's take him in the garage."

Henry shrugged. "Guess so."

"Hey, alien!" I called above the brain-curdling scream of delight that shrieked across the garden. "Come here!" I waved my hand at him, beckoning him towards us. He cocked his head to one side and padded over. "Got something to show you," I said, not caring that he couldn't understand a word that I said. I took him by the hand and led him over to the wooden door in the side of the garage. It was an old rotten one that Henry's dad had fitted some years ago, before he ran off, and it was all warped and twisted in the frame.

It was also painted bright yellow. I hate yellow. It's far too cheerful.

Henry turned the handle and tugged hard to open the door. It stuck a second then flew open as he leaned backwards on his heels, almost causing him to fall on his bum.

I tugged the alien's hand and led him inside. Even though it was a bright sunny day outside, the inside of the garage was pitch black because we had painted the windows over so as not to be disturbed. The alien's eyes blinked rapidly when I flicked on the stark fluorescent tube which flickered and hummed above us, illuminating our workspace.

The alien saw what was left of Petey.

Henry slammed the door and locked it shut.

I picked the large hammer off the garage's workbench and slugged the alien on the back of the head. He went out like a light and slumped to the concrete floor which was splattered in canine blood.

It didn't take us too long to get set up. The tripod was still standing in the middle of the room and the various tools we had used on Petey were waiting for us on the workbench. We just had to roll the messy remains of Henry's old mutt out of the way before we could tie the alien down in his place.

When we were ready and had donned goggles and masks so as not to get completely covered in whatever was inside our next subject, I turned to the video camera and said, "Well viewers, we have a real treat for you today! Not just one autopsy, but two. What's more, look at what we'll be cutting up this time…"

Henry panned the camera across to the unconscious alien as I raised my dented and battered saw.

Sudden Silence

Krepotkin didn't know what hit him first; that
his cover was blown, or the speeding black saloon.

The Virtuous Man

*"He who rose like a dragon of old shall be slain by
the man of virtue."*

The cold air was a well-honed dagger wheedling its way into Jason's cloak, seeking out veins to slice and arteries to chill. As he stood at the edge of the vast stagnant lake that surrounded his Ultima Thule, the dark-haired man pulled his heavy garments around him for better protection. It had been such a long journey, from his small sleepy village at the farthest end of the land to this spot where he would fulfil his destiny.

"He who rose like a dragon of old shall be slain by the man of virtue."

How old had he been when he had first heard of the prophecy, words of hope handed down from generation to generation? Ten, eleven? It was hard to remember in this land where time was insignificant and the seasons drifted to and fro like the wind over the barren hills. All that mattered to the remnants of his race was survival; scratching a meagre existence from the scorched land and not suffering a demeaning fate at the hands of the constructs or their masters.

He cast a nervous eye around him as a sound creaked across the foggy water. It was just the boatman, the one for whom he waited – nothing more. Neither creature made of clay, nor denizen of hell astride a black horse watching over the wanton destruction of a village of innocents.

He considered himself immensely fortunate. He had seen many constructs on his long journey and had witnessed the wrath of the two dark deputies of Kanor. He had escaped, helped by those who knew of his epic quest, those who had sacrificed their lives for the greater good of humanity.

He ran his thumb over the smooth wooden talisman that was gripped tight in his left hand. So many had perished so that he could stand here now with this object. He looked down at the small innocuous token and, as his eyes studied the two symbols that were crudely scratched into it, a cup and a blade, he felt a warm tear edge its way out of his eye.

Now was not the time for sorrow. Now was the time to stick one's courage to the post and set matters straight. Hundreds of years ago, if folk knew correctly, the creature on the island in the middle of the lake would have shed tears. For, back then, he was supposed to have been a human, a mortal of flesh and blood. But now...

Now he was a creature of pure spite. Something had corrupted him from the human which he had been born to the ravenous spirit of an all-consuming dragon, one who had torched the very earth upon which he had walked.

There was a gentle thud of wood on wood as the ancient boat drew up to the pier upon which the pensive man was standing. Its ferryman stood hunched under a ripped, moth-eaten cloak. Gripping its punt with one withered hand, it stretched out its other, demanding payment. Jason placed the talisman into the man's palm. It drew the object up to its hooded face and studied it intently before nodding and gesturing for its passenger to come aboard. The man stepped carefully onto the rocking boat and seated himself down. The oarsman tossed the talisman back to his passenger. Jason caught it and frowned. "Don't you need to keep it?" he enquired.

There was no reply, just the sound of a long wooden pole easing the rickety boat away from the stony shore.

Jason reflected that this more or less summarised his quest. So many expectations overturned. Back in his home village he had been somewhat of an anachronism. He was a cleric from a long dead religion, one that worshipped a dying and rising god, a deity who had sacrificed himself for all humanity. By day he had tried to nurture shoots from arid land; by night he had preached to those who would listen, to breathe life into their dying souls. He had expected that this would be his lot until one day the horde of constructs had arrived with one of the Fallen at their head, the male. They had torched his village for no apparent reason and slaughtered all that they could find.

Only he had lived to bear witness to the

carnage.

With nothing to keep him there, he had begun his wanderings through the lands. As he had travelled, he heard more and more about the prophecy, words that brought him hope just as his faith in the dying and rising god had previously sustained him. He learnt of the lair of Kanor, an ancient decaying church surrounded by a lake which had been dug by the mindless denizens of the black dragon. Jason had assumed that it would be unassailable, that no mortal could reach it. Then he heard tell of the eternal talisman, a token bearing the sign of a cup and a blade that permitted a soul to traverse the lake.

How he had searched for that token! He had craved it, had hungered for it. He would lay awake at night dreaming of it in his hand, taking him across this legendary lake to avenge his fallen neighbours. For so many years he had scoured the land, searching out this tiny little thing, but to no avail. As he journeyed from settlement to settlement, he witnessed and heard tell of more and more atrocities committed by the servants of Kanor. He thought that ice must run through their veins as they showed no mercy, no compassion. As he prayed night after night to his ancient god, he begged, *pleaded*, that when the time came, he too would show no compassion to the creature that had devastated his creator's land.

Then he came upon the dagger.

As the boat rocked beneath him, Jason felt the heavy weight of the blade push against his leg. He recalled the first time that he had lain eyes upon it, in the ruin of a small cemetery not far from this place. It had been buried with its former owner in a small, overgrown crypt. At first he had thought that he had discovered the resting place of the talisman as the cup and the blade had been etched above the broken wooden door, but as soon as he had seen the glint of the polished metal in the skeletal hands, he had known that his quest was true and he would fulfil his vengeance.

That night he had slept fitfully, dreams of the dagger in his hand as he stabbed it over and over into the shadowy figure of his planet's nemesis. The next morning, he had awoken to the sound of tentative knocking on the door of his accommodation. With bleary eyes he had gazed down upon two children dressed in pitiful rags; a boy barely in double figures and his sister even younger. To his amazement, they handed him the thing for which he had been searching; the eternal talisman. Miraculously, it had been entrusted to them for safekeeping with the instructions that they should, in turn, search him out.

His prayers had truly been answered.

The boat thudded to a halt and he was snapped out of his reminiscing. They had reached the opposite shore. The boatman just stood to one side and waited for his passenger to disembark. Carefully, Jason lowered himself onto the muddy shoreline and set off to the interior of the island without a word.

The place was deserted. He had expected it to be crawling with the vile, misshapen constructs that walked and devastated his land, but instead, there was just him and the ghosts of the world before. As he approached the ancient church, he could not help but marvel at its construction. The edifice was the largest manmade structure that he had ever lain eyes upon and he could not help but imagine what it must have been like before the Divergence, before the rise of the black dragon, Kanor. Back in his village, his modest dwelling could have held a dozen folk at the very most; this building would have held hundreds! What if there had been such a building in every village? His now old, dying religion would have been widespread and vibrant, the heart of communities across the land.

Jason drew the dagger from his cloak and watched as its wavy blade glinted in the half light. His time was close. He could taste the sweet revenge that this weapon promised him. Carefully, he approached the door to the church and eased it open. He immediately had to cover his mouth as the foetid stench from within caused his stomach to lurch. Bringing his guts under control by breathing gently through his mouth, he walked cautiously into the gloom.

As he had surmised from outside, a long time ago it had truly been a beautiful building. Rows of wooden seats, once highly polished, now broken and decayed, sat in parallel rows, facing away from a pedestal situated at the rear of the building atop which was set a stone bowl. In front of them was a long wooden screen upon which hung a carved figure of a near naked man nailed to a cross. Jason frowned at the image. This was his dying and rising god. He had never actually seen any image of him before but had heard tell of his gruesome death. On either side of the wooden statuary were displayed what he assumed to be two victims of the resident of this macabre church. They were tied to wooden poles and their stomachs had been sliced open, their guts pouring down beneath them. Their flayed skin had been peeled back in a grotesque mockery of six-fold wings.

The priest lowered his eyes in disgust and he frowned as he caught sight of a small object at his feet, the likes of which he had never lain eyes on before. It was small and cylindrical, the size of the tip of his small finger. Mainly light brown in colour with a papery white end it appeared to have been burnt and then crushed.

He was about to bend and pick the item up for closer inspection when a dry voice called across the church, "Aha! Another visitor. Two in one day. I am feeling quite popular."

Jason's head snapped to one side at the sound of the voice. It was dry and old, yet contained an edge of amusement. It belonged to a hooded figure who emerged from the shadows of the building. The priest lifted the dagger for protection.

"Excellent!" the stranger crowed, clapping his hands together with glee. "You found the knife! I really wasn't sure about that touch. I thought it a bit gauche, if you know what I mean?"

Jason edged towards the centre of the church to get a better look at the figure. It stood beneath the cruciform simulacrum on the screen, its hood obscuring most of its face. All that could be seen of its features was its mouth, amusement obvious on its lips. "Who are you?" asked the cleric.

"Oh! Forgive me," the stranger apologised, lowering his hood to reveal a pale face and dark eyes. "Please allow me to introduce myself. I'm Kanor. Now, I believe you've come here to assassinate me."

This was it. This was the moment. Jason was stood here in front of the being that had destroyed his land and eradicated his people. His servants had committed such atrocious acts of genocide on humanity. His creations had put the land to the torch. Jason felt the anger surge through him and he raised the dagger above his head and charged forward toward his unarmed nemesis.

With each step he came closer and closer to the end of his quest. He would plunge the dagger down into this creature's dark heart and usher in an age of light. With the spilling of Kanor's blood as a sacrifice, the land would be born anew.

He was now a breath away from his quarry and the dagger plummeted through the air towards the black dragon's chest.

Then it stopped mid-air and the would-be assassin stumbled to his knees.

He gaped in horror at the impossible sight in front of him. A manacle of flowing water was clasped around his wrist, making it immobile. He yanked frantically at the mind-bending apparition. How could this be? What arcane magic was this?

Kanor bent down towards the man, a broad smile on his face. "You really should check the shadows, my friend," he said, shaking his head in mock dismay. "You never know what lurks there."

There was the whisper of light footsteps and Jason saw two more figures appear from the surrounding gloom. His heart sank. The Fallen! Both of them! The female had a hand held out in front of her, water incredibly bouncing from her fingertips, a wicked smile on her beautiful face. The male wore his usual scowl of contempt and was clenching and unclenching his fists.

"But..."

Kanor gave an apologetic shrug of his cloaked shoulders. "Your lust for revenge," he explained. "Sorry. Just not really that virtuous, is it? Him up there," he gestured to the figure on the cross, "I've actually met him you know, and I'm pretty sure he wouldn't approve." He looked over at the male Fallen. "Finish it."

The Fallen lifted his right hand and the last thing that Jason saw was a lethal flash of blinding energy.

"So, how long did that actually take, then?"

"Five months, give or take a day."

Kanor turned to his female lieutenant. "*Five months?* That long?" He shook his head and turned to the other Fallen, whose fingers still crackled with deadly electricity. "I thought the idea of giving them a dagger was supposed to speed things up."

"Never trust a man to do a woman's job," the female jibed, playfully dancing pearls of water around the air in front of her.

"Don't blame me!" her partner spat. "You were the one who took the talisman to the wrong village."

"How was I supposed to know he was dying?"

"He could hardly get out of bed! For pity's sake, he was being cared for by his teenage daughter. If she hadn't passed it on to those other kids…"

The female opened her mouth to retort.

"Children, children," their master interrupted. "We don't have time for this. Not at all." He stepped over the charred remains of his would-be assassin without even a second glance and walked confidently to the centre of the nave, his eyes scanning the stone floor. "Humanity is weakening. The end days are nearing. The true man of virtue cannot be far away. If I am to stand any chance of overcoming that prophecy, I need the Eternals in my possession before he raises his goody-two-shoes head.

"And don't forget that, if I fall, he will have gone through both of you first to reach me."

A sullen silence fell across the dead church as he bent down and picked up the small object that had caught the eye of his doomed attacker, a sparkle of curiosity in his eyes.

The Fallen approached their master and looked at the thing that he was turning over in his pale fingers.

"Was he a smoker?" the male asked.

"Not until you did your thing with him," Kanor quipped. "No. I was visited by an *old friend* just before he stumbled in to fulfil his *destiny*." He spat the word out as he twisted the discarded cigarette butt so that the words "Lucky Strike" were plainly visible. He chuckled when he heard his servants swear.

"Good. You now understand why time is of the

essence. Asherah, see to it that the talisman is found quicker this time. Much quicker. Asmodeus," he bent down and picked up the fallen dagger, "can't you tarnish this a bit or something? It's supposed to be ancient, for Christ's sake.

"And let's see if we can get the next fool here a bit quicker this time. It's time that virtue was a thing of the past..."

Personal Enrichment

Personal enrichment. That's what my line manager called it. A chance to develop one's personal skills in a group environment over a weekend in the countryside.

Personal hell. That's what I saw it as. There is a reason why I do the job I do, sitting at a screen cold-calling random people and telling them about suing their banks, claiming insurance for accidents or whatever the thing is that week. It's because I don't like to socialise. Other people do my head in, they really do. Well, other people apart from Trudy, two booths down on the right. She's okay. Well, *more* than okay. She's utterly awesome and we've been dating for a few weeks now. Trudy gets me; she understands that I'm just a quiet guy who likes to be left alone to do his own thing. I'm not like all the others in the office who high-five and huzzah every time they make a killing. I just smile quietly to myself and get on with my job. I push the buttons, talk the talk and tread water until that hour hand reaches five and it's time to clock off.

Me, I prefer books. You ought to see my flat; it's floor to ceiling with them. It doesn't matter what type or genre. I just love to read whatever I can get my hands on. There are even a few copies of *Cosmo* dotted about somewhere from when I was stuck on a train once. I could never throw a book away, not even sell it. The idea is totally repugnant to me.

So, anyway, when I arrived at the centre to be *personally improved*, imagine my horror when I found that I was to be sharing a bunkhouse with all my other male co-workers. Not only that, but I was to be studying with them. There were twelve bunks set out next to twelve wooden desks which were each surmounted by a jotter emblazoned with some sort of sickeningly sweet motivational logo. I quickly made my way to the far corner and rummaged around in my bag for a book. Lying out on the less than comfortable bed, I tried to immerse myself into the fantasy world of steam-propelled dragons and iron-clad trolls, but my co-workers would have none of it. They were too busy participating in homo-erotic bonding rituals and comparing the cup sizes of their previous night's conquests.

I gave up, stuffed my paperback in my coat pocket and left the cabin to the sound of whooping and jeering.

Jerks.

As I walked away from my own little piece of Dante, I saw Trudy emerging from the female dorm. "Hey!" she called, "You had enough already, too?"

I nodded.

"I saw a nice-looking café about a mile down the road when I drove in," she said. "Feel like grabbing a brew?"

I said that I did and we wandered off down the lane. It was a nice walk on a summer afternoon. Only the occasional car whipped past, intruding on our calm silence. We walked side by side just immersed in the beauty of nature - the green-leafed trees and the fragrant smelling flowers, and the knowledge that we each had someone with which to quietly appreciate the experience.

Trudy spoke just once as we neared the café, a small thatched building with wooden flower plant-ers sitting outside. "Don't you think it's strange that they have this high fence out here?"

I glanced to where she was pointing and frowned. Trudy was right. It did look rather odd. There was a tall wire fence – about three metres – running down the side of the path all the way to the café. One could not see too far into the enclosure on the other side due to a variety of large plants and undergrowth, but none of them came close to the fence. There was about three metres from the plants to the boundary. I listened carefully and there, in the rural silence, was the unmistakable high-pitched buzz of electricity. I shrugged and we carried on to the café.

The establishment was a lovely affair. We chose a side booth which allowed us to sit in comparative peace and quiet, reading our own books. The staff and clientele very kindly gave us our space and privacy, only coming over to enquire as to what we would like to order and commenting that it was nice to see a young couple enjoying liter-ature these days.

When about an hour or so had passed, Trudy and I finished our drinks and made to leave. As we did so, I couldn't help but notice a substantial metal door at the back of the room. What was more, the window next to it was reinforced with a heavy grill. I considered this matter to be somewhat curious but ultimately none of my business so said nothing about it as we made our way back to the conference centre.

Back at the dormitory slash study room, I retreated to the comparative solitude of my bunk and started reading again. After a short while, my fellow co-workers started to drift in and I was aware of their usual hubbub but, by now, I was firmly engrossed in my novel so it hardly disturbed me.

What did jerk me back to the horrid reality of my surroundings was when my book was suddenly snatched from my grip. I looked up in shock and was confronted by a bull of a man. He was taller than me (and I am quite tall), rather wide and definitely burly. His sharp blue eyes were scanning the pages of my novel. "So this is what you've been busying yourself with, is it?" he asked.

I didn't reply. I just wanted my book back and to be left alone in peace.

"Why didn't you show for my seminar?" He bent down and his face met mine. I felt like he was a steam-powered dragon leaning down over me, a poor little clockwork elf. His breath stank like sulphur. "Where were you?"

I didn't know what to say. I knew that if I opened my mouth then the wrong words would come out and I would be in even more trouble.

He shook his head. "Retard," he muttered as he turned away. "Well, you can say goodbye to this trash," and he ripped my book in two.

That made me cross.

I'm not a strong man, my arms and legs are quite thin and I don't have a washboard abdomen like you see in the magazines and on the telly, but I'm not really nice to be around if I lose my temper, which is very rare these days. I would lose it a lot when I was a child, but I have since learnt to stuff it away in a box where it can't hurt people.

Sometimes, though, the box bursts open and the contents spill out causing quite a mess.

I flew up from my bunk, yelling at the top of my voice as I barrelled into the rude man who had ruined my book. I lifted a foot and kicked hard behind his right knee. This caused him to stumble and he hit the wooden floor with a loud crash. He struggled to turn around underneath me but his face was just met with a barrage of fists. I pounded into his cheeks and I think I may have broken his nose as there was a popping sound and blood squirted out of his left nostril.

I think I was screaming something. I may even have been swearing, which is very unusual for me, but I was totally out of control. All my anger was brimming over.

I didn't want to be here!

I didn't want to be around my Neanderthal co-workers!

I wanted my quiet life back!

This thug had ruined my book!

Eventually, I felt a number of hands latch onto

me and drag me away. I was forcibly ejected out of the dormitory. Before the door swung shut, I saw the horrid man staggering to his feet. His eyes looked angry. I felt scared. Very scared. I was shaking and I heard someone calling my name.

It was Trudy. She asked me what had happened. I just put my head in my hands and rocked back and forth. "Come on, let's get you away from here," she said. I liked the sound of her voice; it was soothing. I started to calm down and we walked out of the stupid place with its silly seminars and cruel people.

We retreated once more to the peace and calm of the café.

As soon as we entered, the nice lady who owned it came over and asked what was the matter. I told her about the thug ripping up my book.

"Well, that's just plain wrong!" a man who was seated at a table where he was drinking a hot chocolate shouted. "How dare he?"

There was a lot of indignant muttering around the café and I could tell that these people genuinely felt for me. Apart from Trudy, I had never met people who didn't see me as odd or weird. These nice people came and settled me down in a booth, patted me on the shoulder and gave me a large hot chocolate. "On the house," said the nice lady.

I was amazed! I had never had anything on the house before and it tasted delicious.

However, things started to go wrong when the door to the café slammed open and the thug who had ripped up my book stood framed in the fading light. "You little shit!" he screamed and started to storm over towards me. I shrunk back in the booth, really scared. He was going to kill me, I knew it!

However, he never made it as far as the booth. One moment, his face was all screwed up like an old magazine, which meant that he was really mad with me; the next, his blue eyes seemed to fade and his mouth hung open, slack. He slumped to the floor and behind him was the nice lady. She was holding a cricket bat over her shoulder. She looked over to a man who was sat in the corner and gave him a nod. As two of the other customers dragged the thug by his ankles, the man (he was wearing a red baseball cap) unlocked the solid metal door at the back of the cafe. He proceeded to put two fingers in his mouth and gave a loud whistle. There was undergrowth outside, like there was behind the wire fence, and I saw it move. There was a rustling sound of branches and leaves but there was also a low growling sound, like a large, angry dog. The bully was dragged to the threshold and a pair of big furry arms shot out of the undergrowth, grabbing his legs. The thug's limp body vanished into the bushes and the man in the baseball cap slammed the door shut. He slapped his hands together; job done.

The nice lady quickly swept around with a broom before checking that I was alright. I told her that I was and went back to drinking my hot chocolate.

Yes, these people really liked me.

I felt personally enriched.

Through The Eyes Of A Dragon

"So, thank you all for coming today, okay? I know this must be really hard for you, okay. So, to start with, we're all going to just have a friendly little chat, okay, about the things that are, you know, bothering us."

The man felt like sinking back into his seat, disappearing from view, but as the chair was formed from a utilitarian rigid blue plastic, he could hardly even manage a bored slouch. Instead, he was forced to sit up straight and pay begrudging attention to the other members of the group of self-helpers. Those who were anxious about leaving the house in case they picked up the latest superbug; those who had convinced themselves that they were going to catch cancer from the vaguest sniff of a passing car exhaust; those who were terrified of butterflies because they had read somewhere on the internet that they were vampiric little bloodsuckers who spread AIDS.

Butterflies! Jesus!

But what made the whole ordeal a thousand

times worse were the ineffectual, semi-patronising platitudes that the simpering middle-aged counsellor mumbled to each member of the group, as if reaffirming their self-worth could solve the real problem - that they were all pathetic little narcissists who craved attention and the only way they would get it was to convince themselves that they had a greater neurosis than the guy sat on their right.

"And what about you, friend? Why are you here?"

The man felt his ample stomach churn, as if something alive was somersaulting within. He drew a deep breath, looked the counsellor straight in the eyes and began to speak. "It's as if what I see isn't really here. It's as if all..." he gestured to the room around him, "*this* was not real; an illusion. My eyes see it, but my mind does not believe it. What my mind *actually* sees..." He closed his eyes and there it was, the other reality.

The *true* reality.

Instead of a group of ten sad individuals sat in a circle around an ineffectual counsellor who had probably just clicked a few buttons online to achieve a Mickey Mouse diploma, there was...

Devastation.

It had begun a couple of weeks ago, after the incident with the psychiatrist. At first it had just been at night, in his dreams. He would find himself looking out across a torched countryside. There were numerous ruins of ancient buildings which were run through with all-invasive bramble, smothered under a suffocating blanket of ivy. The acrid tang of charred flesh clawed its way through the air as his eyes surveyed the unfolding panorama. A world, a *living* world, had been put to the torch, obliterated; a new one sown on its decaying corpse. Where once there had been luscious verdant fields of crops to feed and sustain a thriving population, now there was an arid, desolate dustbowl. Where once there had been roads and highways, arteries of modern life, now there were muddy rutted tracks which were falling more and more into disrepair as the human race that no longer travelled along them rapidly dwindled into nothingness.

And there were the bodies.

So many of them.

He would be sat in a café, and all around him people would be chatting, socializing, drinking lattes and other such fashionable beverages of the here and now. In his other sight they were all slumped dead against burnt tree trunks, deep festering wounds in their chests, or they were strung up from crumbling walls, carrion birds pecking out their rotten eyeballs.

He looked around the group of wannabe neurotics, all their expectant eyes fixed on him. "...is something else," he finished. "Something that's not there."

The counsellor nodded knowingly, even though he didn't have a damned clue, and turned to the next member of the group.

The man watched as he viewed the impaled rotting cadaver of the pseudo-professional on a petrified tree branch, its lifeless tongue lolling out of its slack mouth. He allowed himself the tiniest of smiles.

"So, what exactly *do* you see?"

The man paused as he was slipping on his grey padded jacket, a futile attempt to protect himself from the racing winter chill outside. "Sorry?"

The question had been asked by a woman. She was roughly his age, he reckoned. Her hair was a tired brown and wrinkles framed her grey eyes. "You didn't say what you actually see. I was curious."

The man took a deep breath. Living a near hermetic lifestyle, he wasn't used to conversations with other people, let alone those of the opposite sex. "Oh," he finally managed, intently studying the process of pulling up the zip on the front of his jacket. "Just, you know, *stuff.*"

"Must be quite terrifying stuff," she mused, "you phased out for bit. It obviously troubles you."

He shrugged. He didn't really want to go into it.

The woman smiled. "Certainly more danger-ous than AIDS-spreading vampire butterflies."

He caught himself chuckling and nodding in agreement.

The woman drew closer. He caught a whiff of her strong floral perfume. "Listen, this place is just funky. No one here ever *really* wants help. But I can see you do. How about a drink? Perhaps that will help you open up, talk about it?"

The man's eyes flitted around the room. The other members of the group were getting their stuff together and wandering off into their own self-ob-sessed lives. He looked back at the woman, her eyes fixed on his face, and nodded. "Sure. A drink sounds good."

Fifteen minutes later and they were sat in a booth at a bar just down the road. She was twisting a stirrer in a glass of gin and tonic, causing the rocks of ice to clatter against each other. He was grasping a pint of lager that she had ordered for him and trying to not let his perspiration drip onto the table.

"So," she said, sipping from the ice-cold drink, "now we're away from prying ears, why don't you tell me what you see?"

He moved his head from side to side in a vain attempt to relieve himself from the sweat that was now pooling around his collar. All he managed to do was cause it to trickle down his back. The woman mistook his subsequent grimace of revulsion as a sign of nervous hesitance.

"It's okay. In your own time."

The man nodded. He looked up at his companion and saw the barren earth all around her. The trees were blackened, charred by an immense heat. There was no feel of life for miles around; no sound of ticking insects, no squawk of hungry birds. There was neither rustling in the undergrowth nor tread of human foot in the dirt.

And she sat there oblivious. As far as she was aware, she was seated in a small booth in a near empty bar. She could not see the desolation. She could not smell the rotting cadavers that hung from the dead branches.

"It's not pleasant..." he began. "What I see is... like nothing of this life whatsoever. It's as if there has been, I don't know, some kind of war. Something apocalyptic." His throat felt dry and he coughed into his hand, his skin warm where his breath came into contact with the flesh.

"What's there?" she asked. "In this land?"

He looked past her shoulder, over the barren landscape, and then he saw *them.* The ground began to ripple, to shudder, and from its depths rose creatures the like of which he could not accurately describe as they were so out of the ordinary - so abhorrent. His mouth just waggled open and shut, unable to locate the correct words. They were tall and featureless, looking like they were composed of the very ground itself. Their long arms hung at their sides as they parted company with the earth that had birthed them and their formless feet pounded on the compacted soil in a dreadful, monotonous marching beat.

They were an army.

They had done this, all this destruction, this carnage. *They* were the tools that had been used to bring about the end of the world.

He shook his head. "No. I... I can't say. It's just too... They..."

The woman nodded, her grey eyes knowledgeable and aware. "You see them, don't you?

"My kindred."

The man felt his face flush, the heat within him increasing tenfold. "Wh... what?"

"It's okay," she soothed. "We all awaken in many different ways. Some of us just open our eyes one day and know the truth. Others..." She shrugged. "It takes time and can be confusing. There was one guy," she smiled into her drink, "awoke to find that he had transformed in his sleep. His arm, it had shot out during a night terror as he became aware of his true self and it had impaled his partner, straight through the chest. He awoke to a blood-soaked bed and a rigor mortice face of shock on the next pillow. But he did not panic. Inside his head, he suddenly had an inescapable clarity, a vision of what he truly was."

The man swallowed, his throat burning. "What did he do?"

The woman slowly sipped at her drink, settled the glass down on the wooden table and ran her fingers thoughtfully around the frosty rim. "He walked quietly into the next room, where her two kids were sleeping, one seven and one four, and did the same to them. He stood and watched as their pathetic lives ebbed away."

The man shook his head and felt perspiration splatter on the back of his hand. He was sweating like a stuck pig. "I really don't know what you mean. How can...? I just..." His eyes fixed on her drink. The ice melted away as he watched, then the liquid began to steam. "What's happening?"

The woman nodded again. "It's okay. This false you is dying. The real one is beginning to step forwards, take control. Here. Let me help." She smiled and took his trembling, clammy hand.

He looked down.

He did not see his hand.

But it *was* his hand. Just not the one right here, right now.

And it certainly wasn't human.

It was vast and taloned. In its gnarled grip was clasped a green stone, a pulsating hemisphere which radiated an ethereal mist. This mist sauntered up into the air before reaching forward, hungry, searching. Then it dived down to the ground in front of him and began to pull at the very earth itself, its tendrils clawing and teasing at the claylike soil, causing an army of the soulless creatures from his visions to rise and await his orders.

He looked up to the woman in front of him.

All conspiratorial confidence had drained from her face, which was now frozen in a rictus of horror.

He peered into her widened black pupils, framed by the tiniest of grey and saw a reflection of the monster that sat opposite her: a dragon.

"No," she gasped, her throat hoarse with terror. "You're not one of us."

"No," came the voice from the man, a voice much, much older than his apparent years, "I most certainly am not."

The man remembered two distinct things as the fire erupted from within him. First was the woman's drink evaporating as its glass shattered. Then, as the flames enveloped her and the surrounding room, he sat back in his seat and watched in morbid fascination as her flesh began to petrify. Her mouth opened to scream, but was set solid before any sound escaped her parched vocal cords. Paler and paler her flesh became in hue until it was the whitest of porcelain, fresh from the kiln; a statue of grotesque beauty which then cracked and crumbled as the ever-increasing intensity of the heat consumed it.

He wasn't sure how long he had been out, but when he came to he was no longer in the bar. He found himself stood at the far end of the street, observing the purifying flames which were rising up into the night sky. A fire crew was there, pumping water onto the blaze in a desperate attempt to extinguish the destruction.

The man just stood in the shadows and watched. He had no idea as to how he had escaped the blaze. He also had no idea as to what he had witnessed in the bar, his hand like that of a dragon using a green stone to create that abhorrent army of whatever they were.

But one thing he was sure of as he watched the fire crew start to pour water on the surrounding buildings in an attempt to prevent the spread of the inferno, it was a foregone conclusion that the devastation he saw superimposed on the world around him was going to happen.

And there was nothing that he or anyone else could do to stop it.

With that, he turned and headed home, the calling wasteland spread all around him.

Far Above The Clouds

Rain lanced down from the blackened sky above, its stinging stair rods darting all over the man's upturned face. He did not mind the thousands of little painful pinpricks. He didn't want to move. He wanted to stay rooted to the same spot for the rest of his life. Let the rain pour down upon him for eternity. Let it bring minerals and elements that would calcify him, turn him to a pillar of stone.

But he could not look back.

He could not stay.

He heaved his hefty bag and pulled it up over his shoulder.

What the bag contained weighed heavy on his body, a burden. Only he knew what was within the faded canvas material. Only he had peered inside and seen the most wondrous things.

They were his to own and his to keep. They were his secrets.

Deep, dark, wondrous secrets.

He had tried to share them with the people that he had left behind, down in the valley. He had told them of marvels and fantastical things. But they had not listened. They did not want to comprehend that their salvation, their redemption, was so close at hand.

So he would leave now, and keep his beautiful secrets to himself alone.

As for those who had not listened…

The man placed one foot in front of another and began his long walk up the mountainside, away from those who would not listen, did not care to believe, the light shale crunching under his determined footstep. Still the rain fell out the grey sky, dampening his hair, wetting his clothes, but that did not matter. All that concerned him was what lay at the very summit of the mountaintop, enclosed within the cave at its distant peak.

No one from down below ever ventured there. They were more enrapt with the tiny devices that they held in their fidgeting, nervous hands. They claimed that these gadgets set them free, informed them, liberated them. But the man knew different, knew the truth. They had become enslaved to the faceless ones behind the screens, the ones who watched and listened. The ones who controlled what it was that the people learnt, what they listened to, what they saw. No one knew who these nameless entities were, nor did they care. They possessed shiny, wonderful toys that promised things of wonder.

They did not perceive that they were actually slaves.

They had not listened to the truth.

They were doomed.

So the man proceeded upwards through the all-consuming rain, his heavy bag of secrets slung tight over his aching shoulder. He journeyed up higher than anyone else that lived in the glittering city down below had ever been, to a place that he had not visited for many, many years. The air grew thin and the rain dissipated as he breached the cloud-line that guarded the distant summit, his Ultima Thule. He knew that, once he passed through this membrane of mist, there would be no turning back. He would be unseen by those down below, forgotten (if he were not already).

But he pushed on for he still had far to go, one footstep after another.

It was so terribly difficult to see as he walked through the cloud. He remembered his father bringing him up here, when times were simpler. "Concentrate on the path," the older man had said. "One step at a time and everything will become clear." And that was how the man had lived his life; concentrating on the path, one step at a time. That was how he had gathered his precious secrets and discovered the terrible truth.

The life in which those down below dwelt, was utterly pointless.

People woke in the morning. They stretched their arms and breathed in deep the air around them, but they no longer felt their hearts beat, their pulses surge. There was no excitement. There was no true joy, no love, no passion. The devices in their hands had removed all this away as they manacled themselves to the people's wrists, drawing down their eyes to the whirling, swirling hypnotic screens.

This was a vague existence, not a life.

And those entities behind the screens continued to watch, feeding on the people, draining every last drop of soul from their withering bodies.

The people did not leave their houses. They sat and fiddled on their devices, convincing themselves that they were witnessing great wonders, when all they really gazed upon was a sham, a mockery of life. They did not see the rivers flow, the trees yearn upwards to the rain-giving clouds. They did not care for the cry of the new-born child, nor the laughter of the playful toddler. They were told that these things were irrelevant, annoyances. They were to be shunned, parodied, despised.

But the man loved all these things and he mourned their loss.

There had been a time when the streets were full of the happy sounds of children playing. There had been a time when a new-born child had been a joy rather than a burden. There had been a time when people had taken pride in a craftsman's work rather than pressing a button and receiving a pale, cheap simulacra from somewhere far across the globe.

The clouds parted and the man looked upwards towards his Ultima Thule.

It was a place of glory.

It was a place of sunshine.

He had passed through the veil of water, cleansed and refreshed.

He allowed himself a small smile, but he was not there yet. The steepest stretch of his journey lay before him and his bag of secrets was so very, very heavy, the worn canvas drenched in the purifying rain. However, he had travelled it before, so many years ago with his long-departed father. They had travelled up as his loving pa had waxed lyrical about what lay ahead, at the very summit, deep in the cave. An incredible thing that no one else knew about.

Something very old.

Something ancient.

From a time that the people below no longer believed in.

The man felt the strain of his secrets weighing heavily upon his back and he wished that it had not come to this, that he had been able to share them.

But no one had listened.

They had mocked him.

They had scoffed at him.

They had ignored him.

They had thrown insults at him and cast him out, before returning to the dire existence that they so craved.

So, he knew that he had to perform the task ahead of him, enter the cave that his father had discovered and do what must be done.

As he reached the summit, the sun started to descend and he saw glimmers of light pricking their way through the clouds as the people down below turned on more and more of the technology that controlled their little lives. He looked up and saw the heavens above, a vast wide sea of darkness, dotted with waves and islands of luminescence that would not be visible to those down below. As their harsh, vicious lights scraped away all subtlety and restful night, they would be imprisoned in a false day. They would not rest. They would not surrender their weary bodies to a deep, refreshing slumber. They would toss and turn in their flimsy, creaking beds as the bright lights wormed their way in through their inefficient curtains. They would awake in the morning, tired, grumpy and annoyed before ignoring those around them on their way to work by plugging themselves into their little devices and convincing themselves that this was how it had always been.

But it hadn't.

And it wouldn't be once again.

The man reached the plateau at the top of the mountain, far above the clouds and he walked into the comforting darkness of the small cave that was situated atop the peak. He needed no light for there was nothing there over which he could possibly stumble. It was an empty room, containing one solitary item, and he knew exactly where to locate it. He just walked with his hand outstretched until it located that which his father had shown him so many years ago.

His hand clasped around the cold, metallic object, its grip perfectly moulding to his welcoming hand.

And, with not the slightest bit of hesitation, he thrust the ancient switch downwards.

The bells rang out from the mountain top. Over and over they rang as the arcane device cranked itself into life. They were the warning chimes, heralding a new era.

The device rose, slowly into the clear night sky

above the sonorous cacophony and the man felt an insistent thrumming from far below his feet, as if the mountain were alive and was preparing itself to speak. Carefully, he traced his steps back out of the cave and looked up at the device, now tall and erect above the summit, its scaffold reaching up to a new world as the rhythmic pounding increased. The man sensed the momentous energy building up far below, from the machines created by those who had gone before, who had suffered the same fate as those who once again had fallen slave to the technologies they had created.

"It's an ongoing cycle," his father had explained to him, all those years ago, "one which can never be truly stopped."

But the man was trying. He really was.

His hair stood straight from his head and the air tasted of oiled steel as the great device charged itself with its godlike power.

He imagined the people below pausing in what they were doing on their little devices and listening to the sound of the tolling bells chiming from high above, wondering what on earth it could be. They would have no notion of what was to come.

Then the machine's noise crescendoed and the man felt a great wave wash past him, out to the people below in the illuminated city where they dwelt, trapped in their technological prisons.

And one by one, the lights fell dark.

Eternal Night

I see him at night.

All around me sleeps, the darkness smother-ing their lives, forcing them to be still, inert.

But in my dreams, the sky is brighter than the day. His radiance is of a greater magnitude than the fiery ball of gas at the centre of our solar system. He stands tall above us all, his arms outstretched, his six wings unfurled behind him, billowing in the raging tempest.

We are so small beneath him, infinitely point-less. We are of no significance to him whatsoever as the universe spins upon his powerful axis. Galaxies come and go; stars are born and die as he stands there.

Eternal.

He is there: before, now and forever.

And, in his hands, he clasps his kin.

In his right is a Blade so straight, so true that it can cleave the soul of an immortal in twain. Its edge pierces the very firmament above. The matter of the universe spills through the hole that it rends in the sky.

Beyond, there is nothing; no light, no dark. All that was and is spews through the bleeding wound, pouring down into our doomed realm. Heaven and Beyond combine with the sentient creature that enwraps them, holds them in place - the winding, serpentine Abyss. I hear its scream of release as it drags all creation down through the haemorrhaging wound into the receptacle that he holds in his left hand.

The Cup is of no great size yet I marvel at how everything defies the set laws of Euclid, of physics and pours into the awaiting bowl of the golden chalice.

I hear voices, songs of the Abyss, praising Him who created it and Him who destroys it.

He opens his blazing mouth, lips of scorching flame, and joins the song.

My heart swells within me as I welcome oblivion.

And there is nothing...

Disquiet Mind

She woke with a start, catapulted from the depths of the recurring dream like a spinning rock from a child's slingshot. She snatched in frantic gasps of air that only seemed to scorch her lungs, whilst rivulets of sweat trickled down her arms and over her clenched fingers which were gripping the fresh white linen. For what was only a minute yet seemed like an hour, the woman sat upright in the unfamiliar bed, her heart thumping against her ribcage, her eyes scanning the room for normality.

There was the oak dressing table.

There was the white bedroom door.

There were the patterned curtains pulled tight in an attempt to keep the rest of the world outside.

As her heartrate slowed from a gallop to a mere canter and her breathing became somewhat less laboured, she carefully swung her feet out from under the heavyweight winter bedding and settled her toes into the luxurious pile of the plush carpet. Testing the weight on her pale, immaculately shaven legs, she carefully heaved herself out of the bed that wasn't hers. She quickly sat herself down again on the edge of the firm mattress as the world began to sway, snapping her eyes shut in an attempt to subdue the overwhelming nausea.

Then she saw his face again, the man from her nightmares.

His white hair was stark against the darkness of her imagination. His horrid orange eyes held her captive, as did his cruel smile. There was a familiarity there. Her dreamstate insisted that she knew him, insinuated that he had been part of her life. However, as reality started to ease its more solid way back into her fraught senses, she told herself that it was just a dream, a random firing of overwrought synapses in a disquiet mind.

Disquiet mind.

"Screw this," she muttered as she whipped her eyes open, made her way, albeit somewhat unsteadily, to the en suite bathroom.

Gripping the large washbasin, she peered up into the bathroom mirror and saw a face that she *truly* recognised: female, early thirties, fashionably long blonde hair (natural, not dyed), dark brown eyes that her producer continually reassured her were winning the hearts of the nation.

The woman nodded, ran the cold tap and splashed some water over the face that was known to millions. Then she snapped open the small case on the side of the sink, preparing her morning lineup. The pink were for heart-wrenching anxiety, the cream were for the soul-numbing depression, the white were for the constant aching migraines.

Disquiet mind, indeed. No shit, Sherlock.

With a slug of cold water, she downed the cocktail in one go, drowning her demons with a mixture of clear liquid and colourful pharmaceutic-als. Then, fixing her famous smile in place, she prepared herself for the day ahead. One which should hopefully change her life forever.

The smell of a welcoming home-cooked breakfast greeted her senses as she descended the stairs to the awaiting dining room. Her stomach growled ravenously. She may have suffered a disturbed night in an unfamiliar bed, haunted by the recurring face of an unknown ghost, but it had certainly not quelled her appetite.

"You're up," her father observed as he finished laying the table. "Come and grab a seat. I'll bring you some food."

She pulled out one of the large ornate carver chairs and seated herself at the table, spreading a freshly laundered napkin across her lap. The furniture was all familiar, just in the wrong place. Pouring herself some much needed coffee, the woman frowned. Everything was so familiar yet so different. She picked up the hand-painted salt and pepper cruets that were shaped like penguins - the ones that she had played with as an excitable six-year-old. The pepper pot still bore the chipped beak from when she had caught it against the edge of this very table. But they were in the wrong room, the wrong house. This wasn't where they should be. This wasn't where they belonged.

There was a polite cough and she realised that her father was stood next to her, a wide oval plate in his hand. "Bacon, sausage, fried bread, eggs, beans and tomatoes. You look like you need feeding up."

His only daughter smiled. "No mushrooms?"

"Of course not. They're the spawn of Satan."

"Thank you," she chuckled, taking the substantial fungi-less breakfast. "It's appreciated. As is you putting me up last night."

The man seated himself at the table. "Well, it made no sense you coming up here after such a long drive and staying in some poxy hotel, did it? How did you sleep?"

"Fine," she lied.

Her father just raised an eyebrow.

She smiled. "Don't look at me as if I'm a troublesome parishioner."

He shrugged and dug into his own mountain of food. "Not had to do that for a few years now. It just pays to practice every now and then," he commented. "Keep on top of one's game, so to speak."

"How are you finding retirement?"

"Dull. I think I might get a job on a checkout somewhere." The elderly man innocently carved his sausages into precise chunks before glancing up at his daughter's horrified face. He grinned mischievously.

She returned the smile and started on her own food.

"To be honest," the retired vicar continued, "it's rather nice having the peace and quiet. Plus, this place is far less draughty than the old vicarage ever used to be."

The woman nodded. "I remember. The library especially used to feel the cold."

"Hmmm. That might be because someone used to leave the windows open after she had climbed back into the house late at night..."

The daughter and father both smiled at old memories and continued to eat in a companionable silence until the old man said, "So what time are you supposed to be meeting the wonderful saviour of Lancaster?"

Sighing, she finished the last mouthful of her food and slid her empty plate forward. "Dad, are we going to go over this again?"

Her father shrugged and innocently chewed on his bacon.

"Look, I said last night that I am approaching Stone in a completely professional manner..."

"My dear, with men like that, there is no such thing."

"Your point being?"

The retired priest lay his cutlery down on his plate. "Tell me what you know about Stone?"

"The same as everybody else. He rose from nothing, worked his way to the top of his profession as a property developer and is single-handedly transforming the derelict Williamson works down on the Quay."

"And what else?"

She shrugged.

"Exactly. Here you have an individual who has performed the classic rags to riches trick, yet no one knows how. There is no gossip about him in the papers nor any online. No producer has ever seized upon any salacious tittle-tattle about his distant past and crafted it into a no-holds-barred documentary."

"That's because no one knows anything about him."

"Exactly. And that's what worries me."

After a substantial breakfast and her father's similarly substantial paternal warning, the woman had a few hours to kill before her meeting, so she decided to go and have a look see around town. She drove in and decided that it had changed very little since she had left thirteen years previous. The indoor market was now a Primark and a number of the retail outlets had changed names, but apart from that the rest of Lancaster seemed very much the same. Its two sentinels still stood watch: the castle dominating the centre of town and the Ashton Memorial rising up from the skyline of Williamson Park. After cruising fairly aimlessly around the one-way system, she decided to visit the latter.

She pulled her silver Merc into the car park closest to the memorial, locked the doors and headed up to the huge, green-domed folly. It was a weekday but still people wandered around the grounds. Some were exercising their dogs, others just enjoying the view, others playing with their infants.

She watched a young mother at the base of the memorial, running about, chasing her toddler. The fair-haired youngster was squealing with delight and clapping his hands with youthful excitement as his mother swept him up into her arms before proceeding to blow a wet raspberry on his cheek. The woman whose face fronted one of the television shows that was rapidly becoming a ratings sensation smiled and...

...remembered doing exactly the same. She would come here with her young son and play on the steps of the memorial. It would be their own personal castle where they would hold imaginary court and dine on the most regal of food which was, in reality, just simple sandwiches of basics bread and low price cheese...

What the hell was that!

The woman started, felt her legs sway underneath her and lunged for a nearby bench where she threw herself down with a thump. A couple of passersby glanced at her with curiosity but none came over to see if she needed any assistance. *Thank heavens for small mercies*, the woman thought to herself. It would have been a PR nightmare; *prime-time celeb has crazy fit in park!*

But just what was that, that memory? She didn't have a son. She had *never* had a son. Where the hell had it come from?

She closed her eyes and again the face of the white-haired man from her recent dreams filled her dark vision, laughing slowly with malicious amusement. She shook her head, desperate to be rid of him and his cold, orange gaze. She opened her eyes once more to see that the woman and the child had gone. She was alone, on the bench, just looking up at the...

...palace...

...memorial.

A sense of profound loss overcame her and she had no idea why. She felt her throat constrict and her heart ache as an overwhelming emptiness swallowed the pit of her stomach. She found tears pushing their way up to her eyes. As she forced them away with the back of her hand, she saw herself stood up by the steps, in the rain...

Someone was talking to her. A man. He wore a long coat and clasped a wide-brimmed hat in his hands. He was apologising, or trying to, at least. She was having none of it.

She shook her head again.

It was stress. It was playing tricks with her memory.

None of this had happened.

None of it!

She was just worried about the meeting this afternoon; her nerves were tormenting her senses, that was all.

She stood up, smoothed out her skirt and headed back to the car. The woman had endured enough reminiscing for one day. She had to make sure that she was running at a hundred and ten percent for her meeting with the famed developer, Vincent Stone.

Anything less would be a professional disaster.

It was early afternoon when she was stood in the reception of Stone Enterprises. The magnificent glass edifice rose up from the centre of the developer's expanding works down on Saint George's Quay, a suitable palace from which a monarch could survey his surrounding lands.

She had popped three pink pills before getting out of her car, which she had parked outside, and had checked that she looked presentable: smoothed her eyebrows, touched up her lipstick. The events in the park had left her deeply unsettled, but she needed to make sure that they stayed firmly locked up, unable to destroy this unique opportunity. She was a professional and so much depended on this meeting. Stone was extremely high profile right now and definitely controversial. As her father had said, so much about his past was unknown, which led to a certain air of distrust in many circles. Her producer was not fully onside with her suggestion that they feature him, worried that she might unearth something that even *she* could not handle, could not contain. But her gut was telling her that there was a real *story* here. He was a true business poster boy who had risen from rags to riches literally overnight.

And no one knew how.

She was determined to be the one who showed the world the true Vincent Stone.

The receptionist gave her the look of disdain that the petty bureaucrat obviously reserved for every other member of the human race as the woman introduced herself. With an audible sniff, the guard to the palace begrudgingly announced her presence over the intercom and, in less than a minute, an innocuous door off to the side of the foyer opened up.

A sandy-haired man of above average height walked over to her, his friendly light blue eyes and easy smile instantly helped to settle her churning stomach. "I'm Chris Dootson. Mister Stone's PA. Let me show you up." He held out a warm hand which felt calloused, like a workman's, nothing like that of the typical office suits with which she was accustomed to dealing.

The woman nodded and followed him to the lift.

As they ascended to the top floor, Dootson filled her in with the usual spiel about how Stone had seen Lancaster as a great opportunity and was giving his all to the city by providing affordable quality housing with decent amenities for the local neighbourhood. She nodded politely, noting that the well-practised speech was lifted almost word for word from Stone's own website.

Eventually, they arrived at the top floor and exited into a small reception room where a middle-aged man dressed in a crumpled grey suit was seated on a sofa, lost in his own thoughts. The PA guided her to another comfortable chair and explained that Mister Stone would see her soon, then exited through a large wooden door which she presumed led to the office of the great man himself.

She seated herself on the leather couch opposite the daydreamer, letting her eyes give more time to the study of his face. There was something familiar about him. Had she known him when she lived here all those years ago? It was certainly possible. Lancaster was not the largest of cities, after all. As she wracked her brain, trying to recall his identity, the man's lips seemed to move slightly in small rhythmic patterns, as if he were rehearsing a speech.

Or perhaps an apology.

The man's hair was as unkempt as his suit. He looked like he had endured an even worse night than she had. This was a soul plagued by night-mares and phantoms of his own, someone well and truly at the end of their tether.

His lips ceased their wordless fluttering and he grimaced as he grabbed at his stomach.

The woman recognised the tell-tale indicator of unquenchable anxiety. "Are you okay?" she inquired.

The nervous man's head snapped up and his wide eyes stared blankly at her, as if she were a creature from another planet. He had obviously been unaware of her arrival and had thought that he was alone. Red veins formed a tight lacework in the whites of his eyes.

He shook his head. "Something I ate," he finally grumbled, vaguely audible. "Nothing to worry about."

Her eyes flicked to the imposing wooden doors then back to the wreck of a man. It was rumoured that Stone was a tyrant to those whom he distrusted, made their lives hell until they finally broke, rolled over and gave him whatever it was that he demanded. Perhaps she was witnessing this tactic first hand?

"I see," she smiled as the smallest whiff of a story reached her nose. "It's just that Mister Stone tends to have quite an unsettling effect on most people. It would be understandable if you were nervous."

A short, hard laugh escaped the man's mouth. "Nervous!" he snapped. "Nothing makes me nervous. Especially jumped up little builders who assume they're landed gentry."

Issues, much: the woman thought to herself.

He leaned back in his couch and peered at her, a mask of superiority sliding over the roiling nerves. "Why are *you* here?"

She made sure that her own "game face" mask was firmly in place and gave the arrogant man her most professional, camera-loving smile. "My production company, Celestial Media, are interested in interviewing him for my prime-time television programme. You might have heard of it: *Faces of Today*?"

The man shrugged in an obtusely indifferent manner. "Not interested in television," he huffed. "*Real* journalism is in the newspapers."

Daylight suddenly streamed into her memory. "Ah!" she cried. "I thought I recognised you. It's Hector Swarbrick, isn't it? I applied for a job with you at the *Chronicle* when I was a teenager, fresh out of school."

"Did you get it?" Swarbrick asked, quite obviously feigning interest.

This particular memory was a solidly real one, and came flooding back in an instant. She had been just eighteen and had explained to her father that she was not going to waste her time in any more education. Instead, she was going to apply to the local paper for a journalist's position. She was good with words, well-read and knew that she had the drive that was needed for the job. Her father had just smiled, nodded and given her an *as you wish* shrug. The interview, to put it politely, had not gone well. Swarbrick had hardly looked at her, instead studying some random papers that had been occupying space on his cluttered desk. When she had finished delivering her sales pitch, he had finally raised his head, looked her up and down and said, "You're blonde. Nobody ever respects a blonde. You want a career in journalism, go and dye your hair brown, then we'll talk."

The teenage girl had stormed out of the horrid man's office. How dare he tell her to be something that she wasn't? She would show him! When she got back home, she researched all the available courses on journalism before whittling them down to her top five. Each one offered her an unconditional place on the strength of her fiery application and forthright interviews.

Not once did she change her hair, the trademark blonde that greeted her viewers every week along with her probing yet heartfelt stories of people whose unusual jobs affected the lives of those around them.

From what she had heard, her personal wealth was about ten times that of the broken man sat in front of her right now. She had left Swarbrick behind in the dust quite a few years previous.

"No. Best thing that ever happened," she smiled. "Made me the woman that I am today."

Swarbrick harrumphed. "Don't remember you. What's your name, did you say?"

She opened her mouth to answer but, at that moment, the large wooden door swung into the reception room and the PA emerged from Stone's inner sanctum. "Mister Stone will see you now," he growled at Swarbrick.

As she watched Swarbrick trail behind the

suited assistant with the non-office hands, she could not help but feel that it was like watching a doomed man being led to the scaffold.

"Good," she muttered to herself, then closed her eyes and took a deep breath.

And another memory flooded back into her mind.

... standing in front of Swarbrick's desk as he ranted and raved about some jumped up investigator who had been bold enough to make a fool of him in front of his family. He was an interferer, a meddler who had to be taught a lesson. He handed her a Manila folder which she opened. Inside were details of his address and a photo of a man in his late thirties. A man that she instantly recognised. A man that she knew could be used, manipulated. She picked up the folder, turned to leave the office of her employer and, as she did, caught sight of her hair in the mirror on the wall. Her brown hair...

The woman fought back the urge to scream.

What the hell was happening? That had never happened. No! Not at all! She had never worked for the mendacious worm Swarbrick. The photo of the target of his anger drifted back into her mind: the dark wavy hair and the brooding eyes, a raincoat and a fedora hat. It was the man that she had recalled in the park.

Who the hell was he?

She rubbed the back of her hand across her forehead, it came away slicked with sweat. Quickly whipping out her make-up, she hastily and professionally touched up her foundation.

"Get a grip," she muttered to herself. "Get a

grip."

She took a deep breath, stood up and walked over to the panoramic glass window that made up the entire wall. Stretched out before her was the city of her youth. Was he real? Was the man in the fedora actually out there? Was he someone she had met and forgotten about?

And what about the white-haired man with the orange eyes?

Her stomach yawed like a yacht on the open ocean when she thought about the haunter of her nightmares and her spine froze.

There was a noise behind her and the door to Stone's office opened. The newspaper magnate scurried out and hurried out of the waiting area without so much as a by-your-leave.

Someone has just watched his balls get roasted on an open fire: she thought to herself and smiled with satisfaction.

She sat herself down once more and composed her mind and body. It would not do to be flustered. She had to be at the top of her game. This was going to change her life. It would send her career soaring up into the stratosphere.

She had been *born* for this.

It was hers to take.

"Anything is possible," came a faint, masculine voice.

She snapped her head from side to side, trying to ascertain who had just spoken, but there was nobody else in the room until the door to Stone's office reopened and the sandy-haired PA, Chris Dootson emerged, a grim smile on his face.

"Mister Stone will see you now, Ms. Adamson."

Caroline rose and followed the PA into the office of Vincent Stone.

Vincent Stone, the living and breathing embodiment of the vast amount of money behind some of the newest and most fashionable builds in the country was exactly as he appeared on the mammoth billboards plastered to the sides of his various construction works. He stood just shy of six foot with immaculately groomed natural blonde hair and deep blue eyes. His jawline was firm and precisely shaven and, as he took Caroline's hand in a firm but not overpowering handshake, she was gifted with a waft of incredibly pleasant aftershave.

"Ms. Adamson," the businessman smiled, "so very pleased to meet you in the flesh at last. I'm a big fan."

Caroline returned the smile and took the compliment with a guarded pinch of salt. "Likewise. I believe there is quite a story behind your success."

Stone spread his hands in a self-deprecating manner. "Just hard work and determination." He gestured to a luxurious sofa and a small table. "Coffee? Tea? Something stronger?"

"Coffee would be nice, thank you." She seated herself down on the incredibly comfortable sofa. She reckoned it had probably cost Stone more than she earned in a year. "Oh, and please call me Caroline."

"Very well, and please call me Vincent." Stone looked up at the door where his PA still stood. Thank you, Chris. That will be all. Please make sure that the matter which we discussed before is sorted before tomorrow."

"Certainly, Mister Stone," the muscular PA replied and exited the room, closing the door carefully behind him.

The journalist caught a glimpse of hardness in the businessman's eyes before he bent to pour the drinks. "Problem?" she asked?

"Not at all. Just business. Milk? Sugar?"

"Just milk, please."

Stone handed her the fine china cup. She sipped from the warm drink that was infused with subtle overtones of far distant lands and her eyes watched him watching her through the gentle steam that was rising from the brown liquid. Those deep blues studying her, trying to discern what she was really after.

Those *very* deep blue eyes...

Caroline felt an intensely pleasant flutter in her stomach and almost coughed on the coffee. *Careful tiger*: she thought to herself. She blushed as she realised that Stone had noticed her reaction.

Following another quick cough, she ploughed straight into her questions: "So, Vincent, obviously, the first question I have to ask is, *Why Lancaster?*"

Stone leaned back into the sofa and gave a non-committal shrug. "Why not? There are plenty of places throughout the country that are crying out for redevelopment, so why not here?"

"So, you're just saying that it's the luck of the draw?"

"Not exactly."

"So, what then?"

Stone shrugged, his horrendously expensive hand-tailored shirt rising and falling with ease over his toned body as he gestured out of the window. "I like it here. I can see the mountains."

I can see bullshit, the journalist thought to herself, but replied. "What about your past? Is there anything in your youth that inspired you to pour so much time and effort into somewhere that is, let's face it, a rather provincial place?"

"My past is an open book. I have never really settled down, travelling from town to city, redeveloping."

"So, would you say that you don't actually have anywhere that you would really call home?"

"Perhaps I do now."

"You'd call Lancaster your home?"

Stone's piercing blue eyes peered over the rim of his coffee cup. "Would you?"

"Would I what?"

"Call Lancaster your home?"

"I grew up here."

"That's true, Caroline. But you've never really *lived* here, have you?" The blue eyes never blinked as he carried on: "You left at such a young age, determined to carve out a niche for yourself. And what a success it has been; a prime-time show and a lifestyle that I am sure you would agree is several levels above comfortable.

"Yet you never came back. Not once.

"Why was that?"

Caroline sat in silence.

"Your father, he was vicar out at Caton for how long?"

"Twenty-five years." The words were barely audible.

Stone nodded. "I believe that they gave him quite a send-off, didn't they? There was a whole flower festival and the church was decked out with gold and white blooms. Then the bishop came and visited for the final service; Blackburn no less, not some paltry little suffragan. The papers were there, even the local television.

"But not you.

"Why was that?"

A memory, a true one this time, played out in Caroline's head. She was sat at her office desk at Celestial Media. She was in tears; her father was in tears. He was asking her, begging with her to come to his retirement service. There was a knock at the door. She screamed to be left alone. She heard the disappointment in her father's voice and she hung up.

"I wasn't in a very good place."

Stone nodded.

Caroline looked up. There wasn't an ounce of judgement in those blue eyes as he reached over and took the china cup from her trembling hands.

"You're not the only one. Look around you, Caroline. The whole world is not in a very good place right now. It is a boat without a rudder, sinking rapidly. However, the rats are not deserting it. They are throwing all the good people overboard to the circling sharks and are desperately trying to steer the vessel with their tiny little ratty hands and their miniscule rodent brains. The rocks are fast approaching and the hull will be breached when it inevitably strikes them, but the vermin have convinced themselves that their course is true and their judgement is good.

"But those whom they are supposed to be protecting are drowning or are being fed upon by the sharks that wait in the frigid ocean for the boat to finally sink, when they will eventually feast upon the bloated carcasses of the rats themselves as a bitter dessert.

"There is no hope, there is no future.

"What's more, people know deep down that this is their reality, their lives. It plays over in their thoughts and, at night, it feeds their insatiable fears."

He paused and looked out over the city below.

"Tell me. How many people down there are not in a good place right now?"

Caroline's eyes followed those of the building magnate. She saw row upon row of terraced housing where families depended upon minimum wage, zero-hour jobs. She saw the derelict brewery, once a thriving business, now an over-sized palace to rats. She saw fine trees strangled by overpowering ivy which had been allowed to grow rampant due to cutbacks in local services.

"All of them," she finally replied.

Stone's blue eyes never left the panoramic window as he stated, "I aim to change that."

After the journalist had left and, out across the bay, the sun had started to set, Vincent Stone sat at the chair behind his desk and studied the features of Anubis in the life-size bronze statue before him. As his blue eyes observed the fine detail of the deity's teeth and muscle, he heard the screaming deep down inside of him. It was more than a faint whisper today; the meeting with Ms. Adamson had stoked the fires somewhat.

He rose from his desk and looked out over the city.

His city.

The voices of thousands long gone over the past millennia screamed out inside him. They swirled around in his stomach, pounded up through the beating of his preternatural heart and exploded through the heightened synapses of his brain.

He had agreed to appear on her show. It was the right thing to do, the *human* thing. Besides, it was time that he stepped out from his ivory tower and showed the people below what he really was.

What he would do to their dying, atrophying world.

As Vincent Stone stood above all he surveyed, the voices within him reached a crescendo and showed him a city in flames.

The wolf that wore the hand-tailored shirt and obscenely expensive suit looked out over the carnage and smiled.

Author's Notes

Thank you for reading this, my fifth short story anthology. It's one that I have really enjoyed writing and it is great to be able to share these little side trips with my readers.

Here's a few notes about the stories.

Angler Fish.

I love writing in the first-person. It's what I find comes most naturally to me, hence the Sam Spallucci books being written in that style. I also love to peer into the mind of disturbed individuals and explore how they can justify their actions, which society would normally see as abominable.

Angler Fish was a product of these two things. I wanted to create a very vibrant image of the woman "swimming" through the crowds with our main character following her, hence the sharp colours of her hair and her dress. I think I achieved this reasonably well.

The Day The Alien Came.

This, to a certain extent, followed along the same line as *Angler Fish* being that it was a first-person narrative about someone who was somewhat disturbed. *Alien* was originally intended to feature in my fourth anthology *Mourning Has Broken* but space limitations meant it had to be put on hold. Also, I wasn't quite happy with it back in 2018 so I shelved it and came back to it a year later, polishing it up into the dark little tale that we have here.

As a fun fact, the garden and the garage that feature in the story were taken straight out of my childhood. The door to my dad's garage was painted bright yellow and was a bugger to open, just like in the story.

Personal Enrichment.

Yet another first-person story! *Enrichment* was also another one that did not make the cut for *Mourning Has Broken*. Like *Alien* it just wasn't quite ready and had to be polished up a bit before I used it here.

I loathe all these personal development courses that businesses lay on for unwilling workers. I've been on a few in my time and have always wished that there had been a monster lurking behind a certain door to dispose of those who annoy me when all I want to do is sit and read.

Infernal Reunion.

So, don't judge me, but this is actually based on a real conversation that I had with my daughter in a local café. I hasten to add that I was bored at the time, so when I started to pretend that I was a demon with a magic knife that could kill people, there was no truth to the matter whatsoever.

Or was there...?

Sudden Silence.

I love playing around with flash fiction, trying to make a story as short as possible. They are great little warm up exercises to get the creative juices flowing. This was one of those and I just felt it worked, hence I popped it in.

Far Above The Clouds.

I think it is safe to say that I am a *massive* Mike Oldfield fan. His music has always gone hand in hand with my writing and he is one of the composers who are my default to have on in the background when I am editing or writing. *Far Above The Clouds* is the final track on his *Tubular Bells 3* album and has a wonderful voice over of his daughter telling the story of the man in the rain who journeys up the mountainside with his bag of secrets. Then, at the climax of the piece, the music just erupts in this beautiful cacophony which I have always seen as wiping away everything below and starting life anew. It is one of my favourite tracks of all time and I urge you to listen to it on repeat whilst reading the short story, because that's what I did when I was writing it.

The Virtuous Man.

Certain stories I write have taken many, many years to evolve. This is one of those. I originally wrote *The Virtuous Man* about twenty-seven years ago for an English lesson back in high school. It was different to a point, but even then it was set in the universe of *Fallen Angel*. I referred to Asmodeus and the knife and I am pretty sure that the character up for assassination was Kanor. In the original story I had the hero of the piece kill a monster that he thought was Kanor but which in fact turned out to be the villain's pet. Kanor then crept up on our hero and bumped him off.

This modern version keeps the same idea of the original, but firmly plants it into the *Spallucci-verse* by having Asherah and Asmodeus on hand as well as referring to the forthcoming *Bobby Normal* stories and using All Saints church as the location. Then, of course, there is the abandoned Lucky Strike cigarette butt which those of you who have read *Sam Spallucci: Troubled Souls* should immediately recognise.

It then, of course, asks the question: "If Jason wasn't the prophesied man of virtue, who is?"

Eternal Night.

Sometimes I plan and plan a story, working it over and over until I have the finished product. Sometimes I just sit down and type, then see what I've created and wonder where the hell it came from.

This is one of the latter types of prose.

I really don't want to say too much about *Eternal Night* as it is such a central image from the *Sam Spallucci/Fallen Angel* universe. I think I wrote it in about ten minutes flat and I will probably use it again in one or more future stories. I just felt that it needed to see the light of day as a piece in its own right before I play around with it.

I will leave you to try and work out what the symbolism means and who the central character is and what they are doing.

Through The Eyes of a Dragon.

This is the second in my *Dragon* series, the first being *Here There Be Dragons* which was published in *Mourning Has Broken* and was referred to in *Sam Spallucci: Dark Justice*. Needless to say, the unnamed protagonist is a very central character in the *Spallucciverse* who will remain nameless for now. I would be curious to see people's theories on him as I start to drip feed more details over the next few anthologies.

Orion's Hunter/Disquiet Mind.

These two stories (along with *Orion's* Child which was published in *Mourning Has Broken*) make up the prologue to the forthcoming *Sam Spallucci: Bloodline*. I hinted in both *Shadows of Lancaster* and *Dark Justice* that there was something *off* with Vincent Stone. Well, here you have it, laid out bare; the building magnate is the head of the Bloodline of Abel and is in possession of half of the Potency. As those of you who have read *Sam Spallucci: Troubled Souls* will know, that is not a good thing for Sam and his home city.

Also not good for Sam is the return of his ex, Caroline Adamson. After using her in *Ghosts From the Past*, there was no way that I could not bring her back into Sam's life and cause a serious amount of emotional chaos. However, as we can see from *Disquiet Mind*, the now successful Ms. Adamson is herself carrying the large weight of her own baggage.

One final note concerns *Orion's Hunter*. The second half of this was originally intended to be an action scene in *Bloodline* but, as I mulled it over in my head, I realised that it just would not fit into the first-person style of Sam's cases, as a result it found its way here.

I shall see you again soon. Look for what lurks in the shadows.

ASC October 2020.

ABOUT THE AUTHOR

A.S.Chambers resides in Lancaster, England. He lives a fairly simple life measuring the growing rates of radishes and occasionally puts pen to paper to stop the voices in his head from constantly berating him.

He is quite happy for, and in fact would encourage, you to follow him on Facebook, Instagram and Twitter.

There is also a nice, shiny website:
www.aschambers.co.uk

www.ingramcontent.com/pod-product-compliance
Lightning Source LLC
Chambersburg PA
CBHW031254210726
48287CB00003B/1035